His Fing
Sliding A

"I'll tell you someth............, husky tone to his voice, and his eyes were smoky-dark, sea-lit. "You scared the hell out of me this afternoon. I was worried about you."

An odd sensation trembled through Kelsey. Had anyone ever worried about her before? Why should it make her feel so breathless to think Jess had? "I can take care of myself."

The small muscles around his eyes relaxed. "That only means I not only get to worry, I get to feel like a fool for worrying."

She started to laugh. "This is crazy. I really do like you."

Then her delight in his nearness and in her own laughter dissolved into something more intense, an almost painful awareness, a breathtaking, aching expectation....

Dear Reader:

Welcome to Silhouette Desire – provocative, compelling, contemporary love stories written by and for today's woman. These are stories to treasure.

Each and every Silhouette Desire is a wonderful romance in which the emotional and the sensual go hand in hand. When you open a Desire, you enter a whole new world – a world that has, naturally, a perfect hero just waiting to whisk you away! A Silhouette Desire can be light-hearted or serious, but it will always be satisfying.

We hope you enjoy this Silhouette today – and will go on to enjoy many more.

Please write to us:

Jane Nicholls
Silhouette Books
PO Box 236
Thornton Road
Croydon
Surrey
CR9 3RU

DONNA CARLISLE
CAST ADRIFT

Silhouette Desire

Originally Published by Silhouette Books
a division of
Harlequin Enterprises Ltd.

First published in Great Britain in 1992 by Silhouette Books, Eton House, 18-24 Paradise Road, Richmond, Surrey TW9 1SR

© Donna Ball Inc. 1992

Silhouette, Silhouette Desire and Colophon are Trade Marks of Harlequin Enterprises B.V.

ISBN 0 373 58615 9

22-9208

Made and printed in Great Britain

DONNA CARLISLE

lives in Atlanta, Georgia, with her teenage daughter. Weekends and summers are spent in her rustic north Georgia cabin, where she enjoys hiking, painting and planning her next novel.

Donna has also written under the pseudonyms Rebecca Flanders and Leigh Bristol.

Other Silhouette Books by Donna Carlisle

Silhouette Desire

Under Cover
A Man Around the House
Interlude
Matchmaker, Matchmaker
For Keeps
The Stormriders

One

When Kelsey Morgan had erotic fantasies, which was no more often than any other healthy woman her age, those fantasies commonly centered around a specific type of man. He was invariably tall, with a strong neck and work-roughened hands, and muscles that were lean and tight, not overdeveloped with the bulges and washboard ripples that came from trying too hard. His skin was weather-roughened and his hair was never styled. His gaze was direct and his grip was strong, and simple, unadorned maleness oozed from every pore.

The men of Kelsey's fantasies wore white cotton T-shirts and faded jeans without belts, or sometimes fishing vests or plaid lumberjack jackets or even, occasionally, uniforms. They never wore bikini briefs or

pleated pants or overpriced cologne. They didn't hang
out in bars whose decor included ferns, they didn't
play backgammon, they didn't go to the opera. They
were the hardworking, unpretentious, undecorated
heroes of the gender: strong, confident, single-mind-
ed, and unabashedly male.

The men in Kelsey's fantasies bore a very strong re-
semblance to the man who was walking down the dock
toward her at that moment.

Kelsey stood on the gently rolling deck of the *Miss
Santa Fe,* the sun baking the area between her shoulder blades as she enjoyed the sights and sounds of the
busy Charleston marina, and she watched him approach with the same sort of unashamed appreciation
she reserved for only the best things in life: a strong
breeze on a hot day, sunrise through the mist, the call
of a gull on a still evening. He reminded her, in a way,
of all those things—surprising, welcome, and well
worth enjoying.

He walked with the easy, rolling stride of a man who
knew the sea: shoulders back, pelvis forward, head
tilted slightly upward as he cast a practiced weather eye
toward the sky. His hair was light brown, bleached almost blond by the sun, carelessly shaggy and curling
with a natural wave around his ears. He was wearing
an often-washed navy-blue T-shirt and jeans that were
faded almost white across the fly and the inner thighs.
The shirt defined a chest that wasn't too broad and
biceps that were tight and lean, and the jeans molded
the sexiest pair of legs she had seen in a long time.

And from that she knew everything about him she needed to know. He was a dockworker, possibly even part of the group she'd hired to load the equipment onto the *Miss Santa Fe* for tomorrow's voyage. If that were the case, he was late, but that was typical of such men; fiercely independent, contemptuous of authority, he would work when he felt like it or when he needed the money and do what he wanted the rest of the time. He had a room over a bar somewhere, or he lived on someone else's boat. He drank boilermakers and bet a week's wages on a football game and could pack everything he owned in a single sea bag. He was the kind of man any woman with even half an eye on the future would avoid like the plague. Kelsey, allowing a speculative smile to play with her lips, took a step closer to see him better.

At that moment two of the workers started up the gangplank, blocking her vision with the bulky crate of electronic equipment that was balanced between them. One of them, backing onto the deck, missed his footing as the boat rocked and the crate shifted precariously.

"Hey!" Kelsey shouted. Her heart lurched as she visualized thousands of dollars worth of irreplaceable equipment spilling into the sea. "Watch it, all right? You see that writing on the side? It says Fragile!"

"Where do you want this?" the worker said, with an unconcerned glance over his shoulder at her.

Kelsey scowled as she examined the smaller lettering on the side of the crate. "In the wheelhouse. Don't open it," she called after them. "Just set it down—carefully!"

When she turned back the sexy-looking man with the shaggy hair was gone. Irritated, she snapped at another workman who was carrying another box, "That goes in the main cabin. And for God's sake, be careful, will you? I hope you guys are better at handling scuba tanks than you are at electronics, or we'll all be blown sky-high before this tub even gets out of the harbor!"

"Hi there," an unfamiliar voice drawled behind her. "I understand you're looking for a captain."

She turned sharply and was face-to-face—practically nose to nose—with the sexy stranger.

Admiring a fantasy from afar was one thing; being suddenly thrust close enough to count the pores of his skin was quite another. Kelsey was startled into a backward step, and being caught off guard annoyed her. She looked him over coolly.

Up close, he wasn't nearly as good-looking as he had appeared at first, but that was not surprising. His forehead was high—in a few years his hair would begin to thin on top, Kelsey noted with some satisfaction—and his lower jaw was bristled with the faint shadow of a reddish-blond beard. Of course, Kelsey had always found that kind of razor stubble extremely sexy, even when it had been in fashion. He wasn't more than three inches taller than her respectable five feet nine, which made him only of average height, after all. He had a cleft in his chin, and Kelsey hated cleft chins. But his eyes, she had to admit, were the most striking color of sea-roving green she had ever seen, tinged with gray and flecks of dull blue, and with eyes like that he could be forgiven a great many shortcomings.

But the sexiest eyes in the world would not have caused her to overlook the breach of etiquette he had just committed by marching on board her ship without so much as a by-your-leave, then sneaking up behind her like that.

"A century ago you would have been drawn and quartered for that," she said.

He had endured her sweeping appraisal of him with patient amusement, and her comment now caused only the slightest quirk of his brow. "For what?"

"I'm the captain of this boat," she said impatiently. "What do you want?"

He looked at her for a moment longer, then burst into laughter. "The hell you say!"

When he laughed those fine, sea-weathered lines around his eyes crinkled in a way that would have, at any other time, been almost irresistible; he tucked his fingers into the belt loops of his jeans and leaned his head back, thrusting his pelvis forward. His laughter was clear and fine and at any other moment Kelsey would have found simply looking at him a pleasure in itself. But he was laughing at *her*.

"Who are you?" she demanded. "What do you want?"

He looked at her, eyes dancing with the contained mirth of his own private joke, and extended his hand.

"Jess Seward," he said. "Some folks call me J.J. *I'm* the captain of this boat."

Kelsey ignored his hand, her jaw tightening. "You've obviously got the wrong boat," she said, "though I don't know why that surprises me. I could tell the minute I saw you you weren't too bright."

"That is not," he pointed out with a mild, infuriatingly certain curve of his lips, "what you were thinking when you first saw me."

Once again Kelsey was caught off guard and once again she was reminded of how very much she disliked that. She was spared the necessity of a reply by the advent of another crated piece of equipment making its way toward her via a burly workman. "Wheelhouse," she ordered. She moved out of the way to make room for the bulky crate to inch by her and bumped into Jess. "Get out of the way," she snapped, shoving at him with her shoulder. "You're blocking the gangplank. As a matter of fact, get off my boat. Go—"

"What is that?" He edged around her to read the stamped writing on the crate. "Sonar? I've got all the sonar I need. You can't hook up something like that without messing up the navigation system. Hey, bud! Get that thing back out here!"

Kelsey stepped in front of him and planted a hand firmly on his chest. "You have got," she informed him lowly, "thirty seconds to get off my boat and lost in the crowd, or you're going to be very, very sorry you even got out of bed this morning." With a purposeful shove, she removed her hand from his chest and glanced at the big diver's watch on her wrist. "Mark."

"Come on, lady, get—"

"Twenty-five."

He leaned back, again with that easy, pelvis-thrust-forward stance, and observed her speculatively. "I'll bet your name is Morgan. Kelsey, isn't it? They told me there would be a woman on board, and you don't look like a Craig or a Dean."

Kelsey refused to be distracted. "Fifteen."

He reached into his back pocket and took out a folded set of papers, tapping them against his palm for a moment.

"Ten."

"I have here," he announced at leisure, "a signed contract between the Graphton Institute for Marine Research and Seward Charters. I think you'll find everything is in order. The only question is, do I give it to you now, or wait and see what happens when thirty seconds is up?"

Kelsey snatched the papers from him.

"Damn," he murmured. "Now I guess I'll never know."

Jess watched with growing amusement and thinly disguised satisfaction as her eyes scanned the paper. Yes, he had been told that one of the scientists who were chartering his boat was a woman, and he should have been prepared. Generally he was a lot more careful about who he leased his boats to—particularly the *Miss Santa Fe*— and he had an inborn superstition about women on board under the best of circumstances. But with a last-minute cancellation on his hands the offer from Graphton had been a godsend, and he couldn't afford to be too choosy. He watched Kelsey Morgan's face darken as she scanned the papers and wondered whether keeping his business out of the red for another month was worth what he was about to put himself—and his boat—through.

He knew her type. Unfortunately, women like Kelsey Morgan had become almost a stereotype for the nineties. They worked men's jobs, wore men's clothes, and somehow had come to the conclusion that the best part of being a woman was learning how to be a better man. Give them a title and they thought they were queens. Give them a little power and they used it to cut off the head—or any other available body part—of the nearest man. Hard-eyed, tight-lipped, all a woman like that needed was a battle-ax to qualify for membership in a genuine Amazon regiment.

Jess had always made it a point to avoid the Kelsey Morgans of this world. The only trouble was, a man couldn't always spot them at a distance. Walking down the dock, all he had seen was a good-looking woman with an eye for him. Her hair was a rich mahogany red, wildly curly, and bound back at the neck with a yellow bandanna scarf that flapped in the wind like the corners of a bright sail. She was tall, and he liked tall woman, but she was lightly built, with delicate bone structure and long musculature. Her upper body was concealed in a man's chambray shirt that was knotted at her waist, and her legs encased in form-fitting jeans. Great legs.

Her face, on close inspection, was not particularly beautiful, though some men might call the wide mouth with its full, bee-stung lips sexy. Her skin was porcelain white—hardly the kind of complexion that would weather two weeks at sea—and her nose spattered with a few pale freckles. Her eyes were brown, which was a startling contrast to the red hair and ivory skin. The hair color, he decided cynically, could not possibly be natural.

She turned the full benefit of those cool brown eyes on him now, and her face was otherwise completely expressionless. "So you're Jess Seward. Congratulations. But as of—" Again she glanced at her watch. "Oh-twelve-hundred today the Graphton Institute has acquired all rights and privileges to the *Miss Santa Fe,* so kindly get off my deck. I've got a lot of work to do." She thrust the papers at him and turned toward the wheelhouse.

"Wrong." He didn't bother following her, or raising his voice. He leaned one hip against the rail, enjoying the sway of the ship and the sun on his face. "As of oh-twelve-hundred today you've acquired a boat that will go anywhere you want it to, and a captain to take you there. Read the fine print."

She turned back to him, forced patience tightening her lips and frustration warring in her eyes. "Look," she said, with a much-too-obvious calm, "I have a full crew. I don't need a captain, I don't want a captain, I'm not paying for a captain. This expedition has been six months in the making and everything has been planned to the smallest detail. I don't need anybody screwing up the formula now. The people at Graphton must've told you we had all the personnel we needed. What are you coming around making trouble at the last minute for?''

"First of all," he replied easily, "you're already paying for my services—it's in the contract. Secondly they did tell me one of you scientists thought you were going to drive my boat, and I just laughed at them. It's a rule of mine, you see—nobody takes one of my boats out without me at the helm.''

He enjoyed the play of emotions across her face as she swayed between temper and diplomacy. Finally she seemed to settle on some kind of compromise and she replied tightly. "That is not a very efficient rule.''

He shrugged. "Sure it is. I lease my boat to some idiot and it comes back with a hole in the hull or not at all. I lease my boat to drug runners, and all they get is time. I get put out of business.''

"That's stupid!" she exploded. "Drug runners don't lease boats!''

He just grinned, not in the least ashamed of the pleasure he took in having provoked her temper.

"Anyway, we are not drug runners! We're scientists!''

"How do I know that?" he replied easily. "Scientists don't usually lease boats, either.''

She took a deep breath, and he could see her muscles tensing with the effort of bringing her tone back under control. "We're a small, privately funded organization," she explained shortly. "We don't have a whole fleet at our disposal yet and we have to take what we can get. I assume you checked our credentials before you ever signed the lease. If you want to see *my* credentials as a captain—''

"Wouldn't make any difference. Nobody's taking my boat out of this harbor but me.'' He moved toward the wheelhouse. ''And I'm not taking it out until I've personally checked every piece of equipment you've got on board. What is all this junk, anyway?''

Kelsey tried counting to ten, knowing it wouldn't do any good. She tried being philosophical, reflecting on Murphy's law and all its corollaries for a moment, but that didn't help much, either. She had wheedled, begged, connived and manipulated for almost a year to arrange this expedition; she had reallocated funds, made sacrifices and even compromised, which was one thing she tried *never* to do, for the sake of two paltry weeks at sea—roughly half the time she needed—and in the end it all came down to one arrogant sailor whose last-minute interference could blow the whole project.

The trouble with fantasies, she reflected as dispassionately as she could, was that they invariably proved a disappointment up close. Which was also the trouble with men in general.

He was prying open one of the crates with a screwdriver, and in one swift stride Kelsey was beside him, planting her foot firmly atop the lid of the box. ''That's sixteen thousand dollars worth of customized equipment,'' she said tightly. ''Unless you're carrying a lot more insurance than you look like you are, you'd better stop right there.''

Jess raised his eyes to her sneakered foot, upward over the length of a shapely leg and the curve of her hip, at last to her face. He said, "Why do I get the feeling this is going to be a long trip?"

He put the screwdriver down and stood up, his own patience nearing an end. "Look, lady, a deal's a deal. You read the contract. I captain the boat. I inspect everything—and everyone—that goes on board. But, hey, I'm a reasonable guy." He took the contract from his back pocket and held it with the thumbs and forefingers of both hands, poised to tear. "You're not happy, I'm not happy. A contract is the easiest thing in the world to break."

For a moment there seemed to be a stalemate, and six months of painstaking plans, over a year of hard work and hope, rested on nothing more than who would blink first. Very few people could outbluff Kelsey, and she had never met anyone who could outstare her. But she had a sinking feeling this man just might be the first.

His fingers tightened on the contract, and a small rip appeared in the top fold. She snatched the papers from him. "You bet it is," she said, and spun on her heel. "Dean!" she shouted over her shoulder. "Take over. And don't let this—" She seemed to struggle for the right word as she raked Jess once with a razor-sharp gaze. "*Neanderthal* touch anything!"

Jess couldn't help grinning as he watched her march down the gangplank, partly with relief—he really hadn't wanted to tear up that contract—and partly with amusement. All things considered, he decided, her best side was definitely her backside.

A young man appeared from the wheelhouse, where he had no doubt been observing—along with everyone else on board—the events of the past fifteen minutes. "You'd have to be Dean," Jess said easily. "Jess Seward. Looks like we'll be sailing together."

The other man's grin was friendly and amused. "You think so?"

Dean looked more like a beach boy than a scientist with his long blond hair bound at the back of his neck, his perfect tan, and gold hoop earring. He wore a length of electric cable around his neck and had a screwdriver stuck behind one ear. Jess reflected that if this were an example of the crew to whom he was entrusting his boat, it was a good thing he was coming along.

He turned back to the rail, looking out over the dock until he caught a glimpse of cinnamon-colored hair flashing in the crowd. "You know something I don't know?"

"Only that not too many people go up against Kelsey and come out a winner. That's one stubborn woman."

"A real shark, huh?"

"Of the man-eating variety."

Jess watched her push and shove her away through the crowd until she disappeared behind a warehouse, and he could not prevent the twitch of a grin that caught his lips. He turned back to Dean. "You ever try shark? It can make a mighty fine breakfast."

Dean returned his grin, but gave a shake of his head. "I'm telling you, man, you don't want to get tangled up with Kelsey Morgan. I've known men who had to have surgery after just one night with her."

Jess chuckled, running his hand with absent affection over an upright that bisected the deck. "I guess I'll take my chances." Then he looked at Dean curiously. "Tell me something. You guys were really going to let her take you out on the open seas, by herself?"

Dean looked slightly surprised. "Sure. Why not?"

Jess shook his head. "Well, it's a good thing you leased from me. Somebody else might've actually let you try it." He started toward the wheelhouse, then looked back, unable to quite let it go. "You really think she could handle a boat like this?"

There was absolutely no amusement in Dean's face or tone as he replied, "Damn straight."

Something about the conviction in the other man's expression gave Jess pause, making him wonder—just for a minute—whether or not he had underestimated Kelsey Morgan. But the notion passed almost as soon as it was formed, and he gave a small, self-derisive snort of laughter.

"Come on," he said, turning again toward the wheelhouse. "Let's have a look in some of those crates."

Two

"**I** don't know how you do it, Kelsey," Craig complained, glancing uneasily around the dimly lit, smoky little bar. "Hundreds of restaurants, nightclubs and bars in the historic city of Charleston, South Carolina, and you manage, without fail and on the first try, to pick the one with the most knife fights per capita of anyplace in the Continental U.S."

"Also the best seafood," Dean pointed out, and popped another shrimp into his mouth.

"He can't get away with this." Kelsey scowled, slamming her mug down on the table with enough force to cause half its contents to slosh out. "How can he get away with this?"

Craig and Dean exchanged a glance, but wisely remained silent.

Kelsey had spent most of the afternoon on the telephone with Bob McKenzie, administrative head of the Graphton Institute. McKenzie was a middle-aged, conservative, business-school type who knew everything about bean counting and nothing about Marine Biology, and he and Kelsey had been at war since she had joined the Institute three years ago. Kelsey understood the need for administrative personnel, and she also understood why it was necessary for them to be dull, unimaginative and compulsive. What she didn't understand was why they all seemed to come with a built-in gene that refused to allow them to listen to reason when it was offered by an expert—that expert being, of course, Kelsey herself.

"Budgets," she muttered bitterly. The word tasted sour and she washed it down with another swallow of beer. "That's all he could talk about—budgets!"

"You're the one who voted to put our money into equipment instead of another boat," Dean pointed out.

"And you're the one who couldn't wait until our own research vessel was free," added Craig.

Kelsey swept them both a scathing look. They had been in perfect agreement with her on the matter of equipment—as had every other scientist at the Institute—and they both knew the whims of nature could not wait on their own convenience. Men. They would argue with a fence post about which way the wind was blowing for nothing more than the sake of argument.

"You know how he found this sea worm, don't you?" she challenged.

"The Yellow Pages?" Dean ventured.

"They were in the Navy together. McKenzie expected a good deal and I guess he got one, but who knows what *we* got—"

"Hold on there, Kelsey," Dean objected. "You checked the boat out yourself. Let's not go borrowing trouble."

Kelsey scowled and lifted her mug again. She knew she was starting to exaggerate, but she resented having the fact pointed out by Dean. The truth was, the *Miss Santa Fe* had passed her initial inspection with flying colors—one almost might say it had been love at first sight. The forty-foot cruiser, complete with a flying bridge for fishing, bunk space for six, a shower and lavatory facilities and a neat, well-appointed galley, had been maintained with a loving, expert hand. The main cabin would provide plenty of room for their research station while doubling as sleeping quarters for the men, and the captain's cabin, though smaller, was nicely appointed and offered more than she had expected in the way of privacy and work space for herself. She recalled observing, at the time, that they had been extraordinarily fortunate to acquire such a boat. Now she knew why.

"I don't know what the big deal is," Craig said, still glancing warily around the noisy bar with its burly, high-spirited occupants. "I'd think you'd be happy to turn the captain's duties over to someone else, and free up your time for your own work. What's so important about driving a damn boat anyway?''

Dean chuckled, and his eyes took on the sharp edge of a teasing glint. ''Now there is where you show your ignorance about our fearless leader, my friend. Why does the man climb the mountain? Because it's there. Why does Kelsey have to captain the boat? Because it's there. She has a little problem yielding to authority,'' he confided to Craig. ''It's easier not to argue with her. You'll learn.''

Kelsey ignored him. She had known Dean for five years—which was approximately three years longer than she had maintained any other relationship in her life, except that with her parents—and no one but he could get away with that kind of nonsense. She said to Craig, ''Put a civilian on board with a bunch of specialists and there's bound to be trouble. You saw how he was about the sonar. The man's an ignoramus and we can't be wasting time explaining every detail of our operation to him. Besides,'' she added, scowling into her near-empty mug, ''there are only two cabins. We don't have room for another man.''

Again Dean laughed. ''And so it all comes down to the bedroom. Isn't that just like a woman?''

Kelsey finished off her beer. ''You have the intellect of an orangutan.''

''Well, it's done now,'' Craig commented. ''May as well make the best of it.''

Kelsey muttered, ''Yeah, well we'll just see about that.''

She caught the alert spark in Dean's eye and stood quickly. "I need another beer. Anybody else?"

Dean held up his mug and she took it, edging her way toward the bar.

Dean was right, to an extent: she *did* have trouble yielding authority, but it was not, as Dean liked to imply when he was in one of his annoying big-brother moods, because she was power-crazed. The truth was that she would gladly step aside for any expert in any field and she had no problem at all delegating responsibility to others who were more competent at a task than she. It was simply that, in most cases and without undue conceit, there wasn't anyone who was more competent than Kelsey was. And this expedition was the perfect example.

Though the three scientists were technically working in tandem, Kelsey had been elected unofficial team leader because she was, quite simply, the expert on the project. She had logged more hours at sea than the other two put together, she was certified in shallow water, deep-sea and cave diving, she was qualified on all the specialty equipment—her closest competition being Dean—and there was no vessel smaller than an ocean liner that she had not mastered. Not to mention that Project Simba, from start to finish, had always been her baby.

The choice of a crew was perhaps the most important factor in the project's success. Kelsey and Dean had worked together before and there was no question that he was her first choice. She had wanted to take two more members of her own team, but there, once again, Administration had interfered. She had compromised with Craig, who was a recognized expert in his field but whose speciality had nothing whatsoever to do with Project Simba, and had only recently come to accept his presence as a member of the team. She was not about to compromise again. Not with a stranger. Not with a civilian. No matter what Bob McKenzie or Jess Seward said.

The bar was crowded and noisy, smelling of fried fish and smoke and sour ale, and it was just what Kelsey needed to take her mind off her troubles. There was at least one bar exactly like it in every seaport town in the country, and Craig was right—Kelsey had an uncanny knack for finding them. This was a place where real people came after a hard day of manual labor, where the jukebox was filled with real songs from the real days of rock and roll, where the tables were sticky and the beer was never light and the cook knew the prime ingredient in good seafood was grease and lots of it. It was vital and alive and a little dangerous, the way Kelsey liked most things in life. The only thing that remained to spoil her enjoyment of a place like this was the afternoon's leftover rancor.

She slapped the two mugs against the bar to get the bartender's attention and held up her two fingers for a refill. Someone edged in close to her, but she didn't give way. Then a voice said in her ear, "Well, well. Small world." And she knew there was one other thing that could spoil her evening.

She glanced briefly at Jess Seward, then told the bartender, "Make that a pitcher."

Jess grinned. "Why, that's right generous of you."

"Buy your own beer," she returned shortly. "We're having dinner."

"So am I. Thanks, I think I will join you."

There was no coincidence involved in meeting him here, and Kelsey shouldn't have been surprised. It was exactly the type of place he would frequent: real beer, real food, real men. She could feel the hard line of his hip pressed against hers and it sent a warm flow of awareness through her thighs. At any time, with any other man, she would have considered the chance meeting a happy one.

The bartender returned with her pitcher and a mug for Jess. Kelsey turned to go, and Jess called, "Hey, Ken, bring a basket of popcorn over to the table, will you?"

The bartender answered, "Sure thing, J.J."

Kelsey's lips tightened smugly. A regular, just as she had guessed.

Jess followed her across the room. "You didn't come back this afternoon. I thought you had so much work to do."

"I was busy."

"Trying to break the contract?"

She didn't answer.

"Well, since you didn't, how about letting me have my copy back?"

"You're not the only charter service in this harbor, you know."

"No, but I'm the only one with the boat you need ready to weigh anchor in the morning."

Kelsey's lips tightened. In a moment of sheer spite-fulness, she had actually tried to charter another boat, knowing full well that the time it would take to trans-fer all their equipment to another vessel would not only be inefficient, but cost prohibitive. Not that it mattered. There wasn't another boat available on such short notice, and even if there had been, nothing would have come close to the standards of the *Miss Santa Fe*.

"But the good news," he continued cheerfully, "is that I checked out all of your equipment, and as long as you people mind your p's and q's and do what I say, it looks like we won't have to throw any of it out."

Kelsey swung on him. "I told you not to touch any-thing!"

He stopped, regarding her with a placid, bright-eyed gaze. "I think we'd better get one thing straight," he replied mildly, "before we get off on the wrong foot. I don't take orders from you. Or from any woman alive."

Kelsey drew in a sharp breath, but at the last min-ute caught the glint of mischief in his eyes and clamped down on the reply she really wanted to make. She was a quick learner, and experience had taught her that men like Jess Seward took a perverse pleasure in taunting professional women with sexist remarks; she no longer found any satisfaction in rising to the bait.

She resumed her progress toward the table, and commented only, in a voice just as casual as his had been, "So I was right. You are a Neanderthal."

"To the core."

Craig and Dean disguised their surprise when they noticed the newcomer, and greeted him quite amiably. Kelsey set the pitcher of beer ungraciously in the center of the table and resumed her chair; Jess pulled out the chair opposite her and settled back comfortably.

"So," he said. "You're heading out to the Falpor Islands. Quite a trip."

"You go where the fish are," Dean replied, filling his own mug and Kelsey's.

Kelsey stretched her legs out under the table, determined to relax—or to at least appear relaxed—and Jess did the same thing at the same time. Their legs brushed. Kelsey stiffened and her first instinct was to pull back, but she stopped, and waited for him to give way. He didn't.

"It should take about six hours to get there," Jess said. His tone was conversational, but his eyes were watching Kelsey with studied amusement.

"Two days," Kelsey returned shortly. "We're not running a race." He wasn't wearing socks, and she could feel his bare ankle, pressed against hers. Deliberately she leaned back, stretching her legs out farther. He didn't budge. Her jeans rode up and his deck shoe pushed against her calf. She crossed her ankles, bumping his leg hard enough to cause the beer in his glass to waver, but he didn't move. And he kept that easy, infuriatingly amused gaze directly on her.

He said, "If it's fish you want, I could take you to a half dozen closer spots. Hell, with that fancy fishfinder of yours on board, we'd reel in the biggest catch of the year."

Craig chuckled. "I don't think you'd want to be reeling in the kind of fish we're looking for."

Kelsey's foot was beginning to cramp, so she uncrossed her ankles. His ankle rested against her bare calf, burning like a brand.

Then Jess moved his eyes away, glancing at Craig with little interest. "Oh yeah? What kind are you looking for?"

Kelsey lifted her mug with a sharp movement and took a deep swallow. "Don't get too technical, guys," she warned. "The man's just a sailor, you wouldn't want to strain his brain."

"Mammals, mostly," Craig explained. "Of course we all have our specialities. Mine's sharks."

A grimace crossed Jess's face before he could disguise it, and he repeated, half under his breath, "Sharks. I should've figured."

There weren't too many things on land or sea that could strike fear into the heart of Jess Seward, but sharks—at least the underwater kind—headed the list. While other sportsmen considered a shark a prize catch, he would cut his line if he even suspected the fish on the other end was a shark; he never swam in unfamiliar waters and even at shark-safe beaches he preferred to stay onshore. The luck he had thought he'd had in obtaining this charter was beginning to look more and more like a curse.

Kelsey spotted his discomfort and zeroed in on it with an unrepentant glee. "You don't like sharks, Mr. Seward?"

He met her eyes. "I like them about as much as I like any fish that can eat me before I can eat it."

Dean smothered a grin. "That's not what you told me this afternoon."

"Actually," Craig put in, "that's a popular misconception about sharks." His voice took on the eager pomposity that was only natural with any scientist who was given an opportunity to discuss his speciality. "They're really not as aggressive as they've been portrayed. It's just that we understand so little about what triggers their feeding instincts—"

"Exactly," Kelsey agreed soberly. "Sharks are no more aggressive than any other killer. And of course, we're all scientists. We know how to deal with sharks."

Jess took a sip of beer. "I didn't notice any shark cages on board."

Dean, who could always be counted on to come up on Kelsey's side when the chips were down, winked at her. "Real men," he replied, deadpan, "don't use shark cages."

Kelsey hid her grin with another sip of beer.

"The truth is," Craig said, "we won't be needing cages. The kind of sharks I hope to encounter are what we call 'sleeping sharks,' and they're nonaggressive in that phase. Of course, as I said, the real point of the expedition..."

Jess was barely listening. The only thing he needed to know about sharks was how to avoid them, and he was much more interested in the woman sitting across from him. At some point during the day she had lost her bandanna, and her hair spilled in wild, tight curls across her shoulders. She had also removed her overshirt, and the plain black T-shirt she wore underneath revealed more than it covered. If she was wearing a bra, it wasn't much of one. The shape of her breasts was soft and round, not pendulous or overheavy like those of a lot of women, and with an instinct as old as the nature of man, he measured them against the size of his hands. Her leg, what he could tell of it where it was pressed against his ankle, was just as shapely as he had imagined. His own legs were beginning to stiffen and he would have liked to shift positions, but he wouldn't, for two reasons. First, he wanted to see just how long it would take her to back off. And second, he liked the bare skin contact, even if it wasn't much, and even if he was doing it just to annoy her.

Ken arrived with the basket of popcorn shrimp, removing the empty one from the table, and Jess turned his attention from Kelsey to the server. "What's good tonight?"

"Malone brought in a load of grouper this afternoon."

"Sounds good." He glanced at the others. "Anybody else?"

"Not me," said Dean, who had almost singlehandedly finished off the first shrimp basket. "I just came in for the beer."

Kelsey hadn't eaten since breakfast, and even though she didn't think she could enjoy a meal eaten in the presence of Jess Seward, she was too hungry to quibble over details. "Yeah," she told the bartender. "Make it two."

When he was gone, Dean slapped his palms against the table with a sudden display of enthusiasm and declared, "Well, little lady, looks like you're in good hands, so I don't have to hang around this dive anymore. Come on, Craig, do you know this city has some of the finest restaurants in the world? Let's go find one and blow McKenzie's budget to hell and back."

Kelsey stared at him in outright astonishment, but when Dean decided to display his streak of mischief there was no dissuading him, and Kelsey would not lower her dignity by trying. He had apparently decided it would be fun to leave her and Jess alone and let the sparks fly, and Kelsey was not going to add to his enjoyment by protesting.

It took no further invitation to persuade Craig to leave for friendlier climes, and in a matter of seconds they were both on their feet. Jess and Kelsey had to stand up to let the other two out, and when she sat down again it was in Craig's chair, diagonally from Jess, so that she could stretch her legs out as far as she wanted without bumping into his.

He grinned as he resumed his seat, acknowledging her small victory. She reached for the shrimp basket before he could and pulled it to her side of the table, scooping up a handful.

"Isn't that kind of like cannibalism?" He hooked
one finger around the basket and dragged it back over
to his side. "A marine biologist eating fish?"

"Shrimp aren't fish," she replied, tossing a few into
her mouth. "They're bait. Besides, I just study fish, I
don't have personal relationships with them."

"I didn't figure you did." He picked up two of the
fattest shrimp and popped them into his mouth. "So,
which one of those two guys..." He nodded toward
the door by which Craig and Dean had just left. "Are
you sleeping with?"

Kelsey had always despised a man who couldn't
look her in the eye, but there was something about this
man's direct, alert, consistently unwavering gaze that
was a little unnerving. He never flinched, he never
dissembled, he just watched, and always, behind those
clear, sea-tempered eyes there was the hint of a smile.
It made her uneasy, because she didn't know what he
was smiling at.

She met that gaze now, her hand pausing only mo-
mentarily as it reached for the basket, and she told
him, "None of your damn business."

He did smile then, openly and quite comfortably,
scooping up another handful of shrimp before she
pulled the basket away. "Doesn't matter. I already
know."

She lifted her beer mug and muttered, "This should
be interesting."

He popped the shrimp one by one into his mouth,
chewing thoughtfully as he made his observations.
"The young one—Dean—you'd chew him up and spit

him out before he knew what was happening. Besides, he strikes me as the kind of fellow that has more sense. The bearded one is a pompous jerk and a wimp besides. I figure he'd hold your attention for about ten seconds. So the answer is, neither of them.''

Kelsey remained silent, though she was amused by his assessment of Craig, which wasn't too far off the mark at that. *Arousing,* she thought suddenly. That easy, steady gaze of his wasn't unnerving, it was arousing, filled with secret messages and silent observations that weren't necessarily sexual but were nonetheless intriguing. Was it an art form, she wondered, or something he did naturally?

If she were meeting him for the first time tonight, if he had never swaggered on board the *Miss Santa Fe* this afternoon and if she never had to see him again once they said good-night... this evening might hold the promise of a lot more than good seafood.

''Where are you from?'' he asked.

''Our main facility is on Edisto Island. Most of us live on site.''

He repeated patiently, ''Where are you from?''

''San Diego. About ten years and six jobs ago.'' She refilled her mug from the pitcher. ''Look, I don't want to have a conversation with you.''

''What do you want to have with me?''

She looked at him steadily for a moment, debating... and wondering. It was only natural, after all, and a little fantasy never hurt anyone. Then she lifted her mug and replied, ''I want to have dinner. And then I want to leave.''

He favored her with a half grin and lifted his own mug in a small salute. "Bad choice."

"Life is full of them," she agreed, and moved the shrimp basket out of the way as the two large platters of seafood were served.

Jess watched her snap out her paper napkin and attack the plate of grouper and fries with a kind of gusto that gave new meaning to the word sensual. Red satin bikinis, he decided. A woman like that, all sharp edges and harsh planes on the outside, would be full of surprises underneath. He liked surprises, but he also liked to take life easy, and a woman like Kelsey Morgan would never be easy in any sense of the word. He had made up his mind on first glance that whatever surprises she might be hiding would just have to remain her secret, because they would never be worth the effort it took to uncover them. Still, it didn't hurt to speculate.

For five full minutes they ate in silence. Kelsey could feel him watching her, but it didn't bother her...except to the extent that, after a time, the simple awareness of him began to nudge her attention away from the grouper and toward him. It was impossible *not* to be aware of him: the movements of his strong workman's hands, the flexing and contracting of his muscles when he lifted his arm, the shape of his shoulders beneath the faded T-shirt—without even trying he called attention to himself, the way pure masculinity always did when it was raw and unvarnished. His chest would be hairless, she decided, and she liked that. He should have a tattoo on his shoulder, something small and not too gaudy, that he had gotten in the Navy. She wondered if he did. And she wondered if she would ever find out.

When wondering began to threaten to take away her appreciation of her dinner altogether, she spoke. "What does the other *J* stand for?"

He looked at her inquiringly.

"J.J." She speared a forkful of french fries. "What does it stand for?"

He grinned in a slow, easy way that managed to look both boyish and a little shy. She was *sure* that was an art form. And it was very effective.

"James," he replied. "Jesse James Seward."

"I should have guessed." She pushed back the beginning of a smile that was more in response to his own twinkling eyes than amusement at his reply. "So your parents had a sense of humor."

He seemed to think about that for a moment, his fork poised in midair. "You know that painting 'American Gothic,' with the farmer holding the pitchfork and his tight-lipped wife standing beside him?"

Kelsey nodded.

"I think my folks posed for that. Whatever sense of humor they had, they used up naming me."

"Farmers?" Kelsey asked curiously.

He nodded and took the last bite of his grouper. "Kansas."

"That's funny." She was being drawn into conversation without meaning to, or wanting to. But it was easy to do with him. "I figured you for a sea-born man."

"Actually I was." He helped himself to a refill from the beer pitcher. "I was kidnapped by gypsies and sold to this dull, hard-working farm family when I was just a baby. A tragic story, really."

This time she couldn't help grinning, and she let him refill her mug. Even in the dim light of the bar those eyes, backlit with a smile as rich as moonlight on the water, could make her want to forget everything except the part of her that was a woman responding to a man.

He went on easily, "Actually I never even saw the ocean till I joined the Navy. But it's true, all my life I felt like I was born in the wrong place, to the wrong people...."

And his eyes took on a thoughtful, faraway look that seemed heart-catchingly familiar to Kelsey. She did not know the man at all, but even before he began to speak she found herself wanting to exclaim, "Yes, I know what you mean!" It took her a moment to realize that the look on his face, and the tone of his voice, was familiar to her only because it reflected exactly the way she felt when she thought about the sea.

He said, "As a kid, I used to watch the wind rolling through the prairie grass and see the ocean. I'd smell the sea in the rain. The barn loft was my crow's nest and I'd spot whales on the horizon..." His eyes returned to her, and he smiled. "I was one of seven kids, you see, and my folks didn't have much imagination. They never knew quite what to make of me. I think they were kind of relieved when, the day I finished high school, I took off for the recruiter's office. I didn't even hang around for graduation. Six months later I was in Seattle, Washington, and I've never been more than ten miles away from the ocean since.''

Kelsey regarded him thoughtfully and with a new and almost unwilling respect. ''I've heard about men who were born with the sea in their blood,'' she said, ''but I've never met one before. Except myself, of course.''

He chuckled, and spoiled the moment by pointing out, ''You're not a man.''

He leaned back, sipping his beer, and said, ''Why don't you fill me in on this project of yours?''

Her first impulse was to respond, once again, that it was none of his business. She was irritated with him for having broken the mood—tenuous as it had been—and it *was* none of his business.

But at the last minute she remembered her threadbare diplomacy skills, and thought it might not be such a good idea to put him on his guard. So she took a sip of beer to clear the bitterness from her throat and replied reluctantly, ''Dolphins. We're studying dolphins.''

''There are plenty of dolphins between here and the Falpors. What do you have to go all the way out there for?''

Again Kelsey bit back her irritation. She hated to explain herself, particularly when the person to whom she was explaining questioned not out of curiosity but of challenge. *Diplomacy,* she reminded herself. She had had plenty of practice with McKenzie, but it didn't get any easier.

She said, "We're interested in a particular group of dolphins. We tagged one of them, and picked up her signal in the vicinity of the Falpors not long ago. Now we want to study how she interacts with a social group in her own environment."

He sipped his beer. "Sounds like easy duty to me. All I have to do is get you out there, then sit back and work on my tan."

No, Kelsey thought. *All you have to do is stay on the dock and out of my way.* But, with a great deal of self-control, she managed not to say it, and even forced a tight little smile.

The check arrived, and that was all the signal Kelsey needed to take her departure. "Well," she said, finishing off her beer. "It's been fun but I've got a long day ahead." She started to push up from the table.

"So do I." He glanced at the check, then passed it over to her. "You're on an expense account," he reminded her innocently.

Her lips tightened, but she was not about to get into an argument with him over the price of a meal. She dug some bills out of her back pocket and slapped them on the table. "You owe me $10.97," she said shortly, standing.

"See me payday." He got to his feet lazily. "I'll see you home."

"I don't need an escort."

"Yeah, well maybe I do. This is a rough part of town."

She pushed past him toward the door, shoving it open before he could do the honors. He followed her out into the muggy night air. "Where are you staying?" he asked.

She hesitated, but only for a moment. "On board the *Miss Santa Fe*."

"Good." He tucked his fingers into his back pockets, tilting his head up toward the sky in the familiar gesture that Kelsey had first admired that afternoon. "It won't be out of my way."

A tiny prickle of dread began to form in Kelsey's stomach. Still, she kept her voice disinterested and casual as she inquired, "You're going back to the harbor?"

"Yep. I'll be staying on board tonight, too."

Every muscle in her body clenched. "You can't do that!"

"I guess I can. It's my boat."

"*I* hold the lease!"

He started walking, his shoulders back, his stride long and loose, his expression easy and unconcerned. "I believe you mentioned that."

Kelsey caught up with him in two angry steps, and stretched her legs to keep up with him. "You can't do that," she said tightly. "You're not staying on board tonight. Go home and leave me alone."

He replied, "The *Miss Santa Fe* is my home."

She stopped and stared at him. Her mind was working furiously, plans and prospects tumbling over dismay and astonishment as she frantically tried to rearrange her alternatives. But when he turned to look at her there was a faint, amused gleam of satisfaction in his eyes, and everything came to a halt.

"Give it up, Miss Morgan," he advised. "I'm not as dumb as I look. You think I don't know you were planning to steal out of the harbor before dawn tomorrow? Leaving me, of course, waving from the dock. You wouldn't have gotten far, but to save you and me and the Coast Guard a lot of trouble, I'll just sleep on board."

Kelsey started walking again abruptly. Her teeth were tightly set and her shoulders ached with excess tension, and her steps were fast and furious. He kept up with her easily.

"How did you know?" she asked finally.

He shrugged. "It's what I would have done. The only thing I don't know is why. I mean, what is the big damn deal? What are you guys planning to do, train those dolphins to bring back nuclear weapons and blow up the harbor? Why is it so important to leave me behind?"

"You're nonessential personnel," she told him shortly. "You're in my way. I don't need you, I don't want you, and I'm not going to have you messing up my project."

"Yeah, and besides that, you're not used to having somebody else tell you what to do."

She turned on him, stopping so abruptly that he came up short, and they were chest to chest. Another man would have backed off; he didn't. And neither did she.

"Damn right I'm not," she said. "One captain per boat, that's the rule, and on this boat—for as long as this voyage lasts—I'm it. You want to sit behind the wheel, fine, I can't stop you. But you follow the course I chart. You run the engines when I tell you and you cut them when I tell you. If I tell you to steer into a coral reef you by God steer into a coral reef. You don't talk, you don't argue, you don't sneeze, you don't even *breathe* without a direct order from me. Now do you think you can handle that?"

He threw back his head and laughed.

"*That's* why I don't want you on board!" Her fists tightened and her eyes glittered and it was all she could do to keep from driving one of those clenched fists into his stomach with all the force at her command. And perhaps he read her thoughts, because he stopped laughing.

"I have spent three years on this project," she said. Her voice was so heavy with intensity that it dropped a fraction in pitch, and she fought the tremors of fury that were gathering in her muscles. "I've put everything into it—*everything*. I have got two weeks at sea and my whole life is riding on what I can do with that time and I'm not going to take a chance on blowing it now, do you understand that?"

His expression was quiet and sober, but he made no response, waiting for her to continue. She drew a sharp breath and half turned from him, thrusting her fingers into the tangle of her curls. She felt like a fool for trying to explain it to him, but now she was compelled.

"Damn right I don't like anybody telling me what to do," she said. "I'm twenty-eight years old and I haven't explained myself to anybody since my parents came home early and caught me on the sofa with Kenny Spitz when I was fifteen. I'm a doctor of Marine Biology. I've been published in three scientific journals. I'm the head of a department. I'm not accountable to anybody except God and my conscience and I don't feel like standing here explaining to *you* why things have to be done my way."

But she looked back at him, and she forced evenness into her voice. "Look," she said. "This is a very delicately balanced project—all good scientific research is. One mistake could invalidate my findings and I've spent a year planning and preparing and making sure there *won't* be any mistakes. That's why I handpicked my team, that's why I made sure no one was on board who didn't know exactly what was going on. But it's more than that." She hesitated, struggling for the right words. "Out there, alone with the sea and the sky and the sound of the wind...you can't always go by the book. Sometimes you have to listen to a different voice, to choose the right moment, to look the right way, to find the right course—and I can't *explain* that. I just have to be free to do it. Because if I can't, I'd be better off doing my research in an aquarium."

She realized suddenly how strange that must sound to him, like so much sentimental nonsense, and she was embarrassed. She shrugged self-consciously, her chin coming up in a defiant, defensive gesture. "That's just the way it is."

Jess did know how it was, alone with the wind and the sea, but to hear her say it, with the dark fire of a secret, certain passion in her eyes—to see her standing there with her color high and her fists clenched, so close he could almost feel her heat—to listen to her, and watch her, was like knowing it all for the first time and the sensation was as surprising as though she *had* punched him in the stomach.

A young man in Navy whites and a girl in a short skirt passed close to him, their arms around each other and their laughter low and intimate. The throb of a bass line from a nearby club was muffled by the hot fog of the night air and the harbor lights danced in the distance. Kelsey Morgan, close enough to taste and vibrant with an intensity that stirred his blood in a way he couldn't even define, seemed like the only three-dimensional being in a two-dimensional world. Her effect on his senses was so strong, so unexpected, that it was a moment before Jess could shake himself free of her spell and respond.

He had to look away from her before he could speak. "People hire me," he said quietly, "because I'm the best. Because I know what I'm doing and I can get them where they're going and they never have to worry whether I'm doing it right. I understand your problems, but I'm nobody's flunky. I'm not going to run my boat into a coral reef just because you say so. When I think you're wrong I'm going to question you and when I know you're wrong I'm going to argue. You might be head of the project, but I'm captain of the boat. And that's just the way it is."

Kelsey closed her eyes briefly against the vision of defeat. "You're not going to back off." It was a statement of the obvious.

"No. Are you?"

She met his eyes evenly. "No."

He smiled. "Looks like we're stuck with each other then."

Stuck with each other. For two weeks, on a small craft at sea... Surely Kelsey had coped with less desirable circumstances in her life. But always before, Kelsey had managed, through perseverance and cunning, to turn a less-than-perfect situation to her advantage, and she knew instinctively there was no way she would ever have the advantage of this man. Perhaps that was why the whole situation disturbed her so. Jess Seward could not be persuaded, intimidated or controlled. The only choice she had was to tolerate him. To compromise.

And then his smile deepened at one corner, and his eyes took on a gentle, coaxing spark. "I'll try to behave," he said, "if you will."

There was something about that smile that was so disarming Kelsey almost forgot her frustration. Once again she found herself wishing he was anyone else in the world but who he was. Two weeks at sea with him...

She turned away. "We don't have many options do we?"

"Not from where I'm standing."

She took a breath. "All right." Reluctantly she looked back at him. "I guess I can live with it. As long as we both understand who's boss."

He smiled again, and there was no mistaking the secret satisfaction behind the twinkle in his eyes. "Oh, I think we both understand that."

And, with a small, polite gesture of his hand, he gestured the way forward, and fell into step beside her.

Three

In Charleston in July the temperature rarely dropped below eighty degrees even after sunset. Three blocks into the quarter-mile walk back to the marina Kelsey could feel perspiration pool between her breasts and on the back of her neck, dampening her hair. It was perhaps the close, still night, the enveloping steaminess of the air, that made her so intensely aware of the man who walked next to her.

Without saying a word, without even looking at her, he challenged her. Being with him was an exercise in heightened sensory awareness. She imagined it was much like the way a boxer must feel whenever he steps into the ring—every muscle ready, blood pumping, skin tingling. He had settled into a stride that matched hers perfectly, and he walked so close that his arm occasionally brushed hers. She could have moved away but she didn't, and every time she felt the accidental touch of his skin against hers her nerves flared into a new burst of receptive awareness. She wasn't sure whether it was wariness or pleasure that caused this reaction, and she had a feeling it was a combination of both. She did know that the next two weeks were going to be anything but easy.

The first thing she was going to do when she reached the *Miss Santa Fe,* Kelsey decided, was go for a dip in the Atlantic. A cold shower would have been better, but the tepid ocean would have to do.

When he spoke the sound of his voice was so unexpected, yet at the same time so much a part of the thick, lazy night that surrounded them, that at first the words had no meaning. "What the hell is a sleeping shark?" he said.

It took her a moment to transform herself from a woman to a scientist. "Oh. That's just a term we use to refer to sharks at rest. It used to be thought that sharks had to swim to stay alive—you know the old saying, all sharks do is swim, eat and reproduce. But some years back a certain species of shark were found in what appeared to be a state of hibernation in some underwater caves, and they were nicknamed sleeping sharks. Since then, other species have been discovered in much the same state, and now we're trying to prove that all sharks are capable of 'sleep.' Craig thinks the caves off the Falpors might be a good place to find tiger sharks at rest.''

"What does that have to do with dolphins?"

He sounded really interested, which surprised Kelsey. Most men weren't interested in anything outside themselves, and they never encouraged her to talk about her work.

"Nothing, really. But I could only get the funds I need for this project if I double-headed it—two birds with one stone, so to speak. I picked Craig mostly because if he doesn't find anything it'll free up more of his time to work with me. And he's not going to find anything."

Jess chuckled softly. "Pretty slick, for a woman. And what does old Craig think about this?"

"I'm the boss," she reminded him deliberately. "He's lucky he got to come along at all." She shrugged. "Besides, he'll get what he needs to log field time, and that's all he wants."

"Sounds like you've got it all under control."

"I always do."

He slid a glance in her direction, which was either admiring or mocking—in the dark she could not be sure. "That I can believe."

They reached the *Miss Santa Fe,* her prow reflected gracefully in the lights of a nearby houseboat, her hull lost in the shadows of night and water. She was a beautiful sight, and Kelsey envied Jess, briefly and intensely, his ownership.

Kelsey preceded Jess on board and went immediately to the wheelhouse, flipping on the switch that controlled the inboard water pump, and powering up the generator that supplied electricity to the cabins. She did this instinctively, moving around the bridge with the innate familiarity born of long experience with boats and all their components, and she was not aware of the peculiar expression with which Jess watched her until she turned and almost bumped into him.

"Come on," she said impatiently, "you're not really going to stay here tonight are you?"

"I told you, I live here."

There was an oddly speculative expression on his face that made Kelsey wish for a little more light, to better read what he was thinking. It also made her think about the long hours of the night ahead, and the possibilities that danced around the edges of her mind were impossible to ignore.

She said abruptly, "Fine. Suit yourself. I'm going for a swim."

"Keep it quiet, will you?" he requested pleasantly. "If we're pulling out at dawn, I think I'll hit the sack."

Kelsey moved through the wheelhouse, which adjoined the forward sleeping quarters, acutely aware of Jess dogging her steps. When she pushed open the door of the cabin and switched on the light he was right behind her, and she turned on him.

"What?" she demanded.

He smiled and gestured inside. "My quarters."

Kelsey looked inside the room. In the middle of the neatly made, double bunk was a seabag that hadn't been there when she had unpacked her gear that morning. She crossed over to the bed, swept up the bag, and thrust it into his arms, hard.

"Not anymore," she said.

His eyes twinkled. "Ah, the never-ending battle of the sexes. Can you explain to me why it's always the man who gets kicked out of his bed whenever there's the least little disagreement over territory?"

She held his gaze. "Simple. You're not paying fourteen hundred dollars a night for the privilege of sleeping in it."

He considered that for a moment. "Right." He swung the strap of the seabag over his shoulder and turned to go.

"Make sure you've got everything," she warned him. "You don't want to come sneaking back here in the middle of the night, I promise you."

"Don't tell me. You have a black belt in karate."

"I have," she corrected, unsmiling, "a .22 caliber pistol. And I'm a dead shot."

He looked at her for a moment, then a slow grin curved his lips. "I'll just bet you are."

He closed the door, politely but firmly, behind him.

Kelsey turned back into the cabin, smiling for no particular reason. Irritating, exasperating, challenging ... but exciting. It was too bad she didn't have the time, or the energy, to spare on finding out what else Jess Seward could be.

Had she been alone, she would have taken her swim in the nude. The marina was dark and the nearest boat was too far away for its occupants to be able to see what she was doing—not that she cared whether they did or not. But she wasn't alone, so she stepped into her plain one-piece swimsuit and went back on deck. Jess was nowhere to be seen, and she tried to ignore the small twinge of disappointment she felt.

A dive from the boat into the dark, untested waters would have been foolish, so she used the ladder to descend. The water was only a little cooler than bathwater, but those few degrees were wonderfully refreshing. She dropped below the surface, immersing thoroughly, then plunged to the top again, shaking the sting of salt out of her eyes. She swam once around the boat, then floated for a while, suffused by the silence and the buoyancy of the ocean, letting her mind go blank and her body relax. Here, in the world she loved best, she was completely content.

The night air was still muggy, but it felt good on her wet skin as she climbed the ladder again. When she reached the top a strong hand closed around her forearm, helping her on board. Her heart was beating a little faster than the mild exercise should warrant when, bracing her hands for a moment against Jess's shoulders, she swung her feet onto the deck.

"I thought you were going to bed," she said.

"Never swim alone," he replied, "especially at night. A full-grown Marine Biologist like you should know that."

Kelsey caught back her hair in one hand and wrung the water from its ends with a deft twisting motion. "Your concern for my safety is touching. Especially since I can't help suspecting you'd be a lot happier if I drowned."

His eyes took on a teasing spark. "What makes you say that?"

He had changed from jeans into a pair of bleached denim cutoffs whose frayed ends struck him mid-thigh; sleeping attire, Kelsey supposed. His legs were as tan as the rest of him, the hamstrings and ankle tendons clearly defined, calf muscles athletically sculpted. She knew instinctively that he was wearing nothing at all beneath those cutoffs.

Kelsey reached for the shirt she had left draped over the rail and pulled it on, then was immediately annoyed with herself for the false modesty. She spent half her life in swimsuits, and she never felt the need to cover herself in front of her colleagues. Already Jess Seward was beginning to cramp her style.

But when she turned around, lifting her wet hair from beneath the collar of the shirt, she saw the way Jess's eyes moved over her—from breast to thigh to the tips of her toes and back again—with slow, expert appreciation, and she felt a foolish impulse to button the shirt to the neck.

Instead, she met his eyes and she demanded coolly, "Did you find what you were looking for? Are all my body parts in place?"

She had the satisfaction of seeing him, just for a moment, taken aback, and his grin was a little embarrassed. "As far as I can tell," he admitted.

"Good." She moved toward the wheelhouse. "That's one thing we don't have to worry about anymore, isn't it?"

He followed her, and there was no amusement in his voice at all now. "Do you know what I don't like about women like you?"

"I give up, what?"

She sat down at the small shelf that served as a workstation and turned on the weather radio.

"A man never knows how to act around you."

The wheelhouse was small, but it should have accommodated two comfortably. With Jess inside, it seemed much too crowded. There was no place Kelsey could turn without resting her eyes on a half-clothed thigh or a lean, perfectly muscled hip, and the little room, already muggy, seemed even closer with the addition of his body heat.

"If I treat you like a man," he continued, "I get accused of being insensitive, or worse." He rested one hand on the back of her chair, leaning his thigh against the shelf only an inch or two from her arm. "If I so much as pay you a compliment, you complain I'm treating you like a sex object. A man can't win. Surface temperature eighty-three degrees," he added, "Winds southeast six-to-eight."

Kelsey stopped searching for the frequency and turned the radio off. "First," she said reaching for the navigational charts he kept stored in a cubbyhole above the shelf, "there's no such thing as a sensitive man. Secondly, I like a good compliment as much as the next person." She unfolded the charts and glanced at them briefly. "Your charts are out-of-date."

"What?" He leaned over her shoulder. "What are you talking about? I keep—"

"Third..." She refolded the charts and returned them to their cubbyhole. "I don't mind in the least being treated like a sex object..." She glanced at the length of his thigh, which was so close she could hardly see anything else. "As long as you don't."

She could feel his smile, slow, surprised and appreciative, just as clearly as she could feel the warm brush of his breath on her neck. Both made her skin prickle.

He straightened up slowly and said, "Deal."

Kelsey reached for another set of charts and unfolded them on the shelf. "These are the latest pictures from Seasat, and our charts have been updated to reflect them. Those are what we'll be using on this voyage. You might want to study them." She stood.

He took one small step backward to allow her to move around him, but still her torso brushed against his when she stood. It was hardly a whisper of contact, not even enough for her swimsuit to dampen his shirt, yet a chemical jolt of awareness went through Kelsey, tightening her nipples and heating her skin in a thoroughly uncomfortable way.

He just stood there, smiling, as aware of their closeness as she was. And he said, "Don't you want to hear the compliment?"

Kelsey took that opportunity to turn for the door. "What?"

"You've got great legs."

She hesitated, but she couldn't resist. She glanced back at him briefly, allowing herself the luxury of a small, completely unstrained smile, and replied, "So do you."

She could feel him watching her as she opened the door to her sleeping quarters and went inside, and she didn't mind. Not at all.

Jess opened up a deck chair, spread out his sleeping bag on top of it, and settled back. He often slept on deck on hot summer nights, and the lack of a bed was no hardship to him. But he wasn't sleepy. He was keyed up with anticipation, the way he always was the night before a voyage, anxious for the sun to be up so he could be on his way. But tonight there was something more.

Kelsey Morgan. He had known she was a dangerous woman the moment he saw her. Usually he had no trouble whatsoever resisting that kind of trouble; there were too many pleasant, easygoing women around for him to go out of his way to get tangled up with a shark. But the way she talked, and the way she looked at him, boldly, assessively, and completely without guile... And the way she marched on board his boat and took over without so much as a "please" or "thank-you," as though she had been doing exactly that for all of her life... Was there something wrong with him, that he should find that kind of brisk competence more attractive than it was threatening?

There was, he decided, something wrong with any man who would find anything about Kelsey Morgan attractive. Except for that lean, strong body and that wild hair and that delicate white skin and those lips that looked as though they were waiting to be kissed, thoroughly and often, there was nothing physically appealing about her at all. The fact that she exuded sexuality the way other women drenched themselves in perfume, and the way her eyes glowed with passion when she talked about her work and the way her chin jutted out stubbornly when he nudged her too far...those things were easy to ignore. She wasn't, by any stretch of the imagination, his type of woman.

And even if she had been, he wasn't free to do anything about it on this voyage. She was a client, and he had a business to protect. He supposed he should be grateful for that.

He wondered what she wore to bed. A man's T-shirt, perhaps, that was just long enough to cover her bottom, and nothing underneath. Or one of those tailored satin nightshirts that was slit up the sides from hem to hip. Or maybe nothing at all.

Jess's relationships with women were very simple, and at the same time had always proven to be the singularly most disappointing aspect of his life. All he asked from a woman was that she be pleasant and accommodating; in return he gave her the same thing. But what that same woman might want from him he had never been able to figure out. He knew only that it was invariably more than he was able to give.

He had enough trouble with ordinary women, the kind he could enjoy and forget when the passion wore thin. Kelsey Morgan was not an ordinary woman, and she was definitely not the kind of woman who would be easily forgotten. That was the real danger. So what was he doing lying wakeful in the middle of the night, wondering what she wore to bed?

It was crazy. Impatiently, he got up and went into the wheelhouse, where, after some rummaging around, he found a package of mostly stale corn chips. He really would have liked a beer, but he didn't want to go down to the galley. She might still be awake, and he didn't want to run into her, not at this hour of the night, not wearing...whatever it was she might be wearing.

Better safe then sorry, and unless he was very careful with Kelsey Morgan, he knew he would be very, very sorry indeed.

Kelsey took a quick shower to rinse the seawater out of her hair, but no sooner had she returned to the cabin than she began to appreciate the disadvantages of a dramatic exit. She wasn't tired. She was never able to sleep the night before a trip, and when that trip was a sea voyage—particularly this one, for which she had waited so long and worked so hard—her excitement made that of a child on Christmas Eve pale by comparison. If Dean and Craig had been here she would have kept them up all night talking, planning, reviewing their research and speculating on every contingency—which was probably why they were not here.

The cabin was neat and undistinguished, and certainly did not look like the place anyone could call home. There were the usual built-in storage cabinets and desk, and the only decoration on the walls was a framed print of an old-world map. The bed was obviously custom-built, wider than most, with a mahogany headboard and footboard. Beneath it were more built-in cabinets, and it was made with a plain brown blanket and white sheets—clean, crisp sheets, hospital corners. Perfectly shipshape. There was only one pillow.

A little ashamed of her curiosity, Kelsey began to open cabinets and peek into shelves. There was nothing there she hadn't placed there herself, nothing at all to indicate what kind of man called this place home. Kelsey had never considered her life-style particularly lavish, but even her dormitory apartment at the Institute had a few signs of personality—a framed seascape, a collection of favorite snapshots, the awards she'd won. Not to mention the fact that no one, for any reason, had the right to be this *neat*. So either he was lying about living on board, or he lived an incredibly Spartan existence.

Of course it was none of her concern how he lived, or where. Impatient with herself, she got into bed and turned out the light.

It was hot inside, even with the porthole open. Kelsey tossed back the blanket, then the sheet, twisting and turning in a vain attempt to get comfortable. Not a breeze stirred. The sound of the water lapping against the hull should have been soothing, and at any other time it would have been. But Kelsey kept listening for the sound of footsteps. Had he gone below already? Had he left the boat after all?

Her hair, already damp from the swim and the shower, seemed to give off steam. Her skin felt sticky, and she couldn't close her eyes without scraps of the evening with Jess floating back to her, pieces of conversation, a glance or a slow, lazy grin, even the anger she'd felt when she knew her plans were thwarted, and the way her stomach muscles tightened with pleasured surprise when she felt his hand close around her arm, helping her out of the water. He had a very strong grip.

At last, with a mumbled oath of frustration, she gave up and turned on the light. She picked out a file folder and took it to bed with her, hoping that rereading the words she knew by heart would eventually make her sleepy.

But she couldn't even concentrate long enough to tire her eyes. She wanted to talk to somebody, she wanted to *do* something. Dawn couldn't come soon enough.

She got out of bed and pinned her hair on top of her head, relieving her neck of its weight. Even that small concession made her feel a little cooler, but she knew she couldn't stay inside. After a moment she pulled on a pair of boxer shorts and a loose, sleeveless T-shirt, and went barefoot into the wheelhouse. The ice had melted in the cooler she had stowed there that morning, but she did not want to go down to the galley and run the risk of meeting Jess. She selected a tepid can of cola and moved outside. At least on deck it would be cooler, and maybe Craig and Dean had returned.

Kelsey was a little ashamed of the part of her that hoped they had not.

Four

_____

Kelsey heard the soft rhythmic slap and the louder scurry of fish breaking the water, and she saw the silhouette of a man near the bow. She knew it was neither Craig nor Dean, but she had no intention of turning back.

She peeled back the tab of her soft drink as she approached, and the soft hissing sound it made gave him notice of her presence. He was leaning against the rail, tossing corn chips to the fish one by one, and he didn't glance at her until she rested her elbows on the rail beside him.

It was a little cooler, and the steaminess had been lifted from the cloak of the night. Below them the water was as dark as a rippled sheet of obsidian, around them most of the other boats were still and silent, and in the distance the lights of Charleston were blurred and scattered, like a faraway memory. This was the perfect time of night: the air, scented with brine and fish, seemed to hold a plethora of possibilities, the sky was moonless and big with mystery, and the sea went on forever.

"If I had my way," Kelsey said softly, "I'd weigh anchor right now."

"That'd be one order I'd be glad to obey."

Jess emptied the last few crumbs from the bag over the rail, and Kelsey smiled as she watched the water below erupt into a frenzy of bubbles and ripples as the small fish scurried to the surface.

Jess crumpled up the bag and tossed it into the trash bin that was tied against the rail. "Where are the boys?"

She sipped from the can. "Probably spending the night at some fancy hotel somewhere. They're like children when it comes to expense accounts."

"So. It's just you and me, then."

Maybe he meant nothing by that, maybe he meant everything. He was facing away from her now, his back against the rail, his ankles crossed negligently. But he was close enough to make her breath catch, just for a moment, when he said that.

If she had raised her eyes to him then, or even moved, just a fraction closer, she might have found out exactly what he meant. But the night was too thick with promise to take a chance on such dangerous games, and her adrenaline was already running too high. So she told herself not to be an idiot, kept her eyes fixed on the dark surface of the water, and took another sip from the can. She said, conversationally, "Why the *Miss Santa Fe?*"

"Ah, that."

Kelsey risked a glance at him, and saw a reminiscent smile curve his lips in the dark. He had a great profile, particularly as silhouetted against the vastness of the sea and the darkness of the night. With his head tilted to catch the faintest possibility of a breeze, and his eyes gentled with a smile and the material of his shorts pulled taut across his pelvis as he leaned back against the rail, the only word for him was sexy. Kelsey could have spent the rest of the night just looking at him.

"I named her after the first woman I ever loved," he said. He glanced down at her, and at her expression, insisted, "No kidding. I was about thirteen, I saw a picture of Miss Santa Fe in a Feed and Seed catalog or something, and it was love at first sight. I tore out the picture and hung it on my wall where it stayed until it got so dry and old little pieces of it started falling off every time somebody walked by. I used to kiss it for luck every time I had an exam or a big game, and she never failed me once. This *Miss Santa Fe* has been just about as lucky."

"How many boats do you own?"

He hesitated. "Until last year, six. When the partnership dissolved, I kept the *Miss Santa Fe,* my serious party boat, and the *Little Phoenix,* for bread-and-butter fishing charters. He got the rest."

Kelsey commented, "Sounds like a divorce settlement, and you were the one who was screwing around."

He laughed softly. "Yeah, it does, doesn't it? But the truth is, we both got what we wanted. He got the four tour boats, a big staff and a downtown office. I got the *Miss Santa Fe*, a little cash, and not to have a partner anymore."

Kelsey shook her head. "It's still not very efficient. You've got the *Little Phoenix* sitting idle for two weeks while you take us out, when if you'd let me do it my way, you could be collecting fees on both boats..."

"That's exactly," he reminded her pointedly, "why I don't have a partner anymore."

"Because he tried to make a profit?"

"Because he tried to take over."

Kelsey could have replied to that, but chose instead, diplomatically, to sip her drink. "Where do you really live?"

"What is this, twenty questions?"

She felt a little defensive, and it showed. She wasn't good with idle talk, cocktail-party chatter, or getting-to-know-you dialogue, and she didn't want to find herself trapped in one of those awkward conversational quagmires. She shrugged, and brought the soft drink to her lips again, not looking at him. "Forget I asked."

"No, I don't mind. I'll play. As long as I get to ask you a few questions of my own."

She glanced at him speculatively, considering. "You can ask," she decided.

He grinned, and the spark in his eye sent a little shiver of pleasure down Kelsey's spine.

"I told you," he answered, "I live wherever I happen to be. Here, or on the *Little Phoenix,* or at my office. I'll bet that bothers you. Most women can't understand a man who doesn't need a home."

"Nope." Kelsey lifted the can again, gazing out over the marina. "I was just wondering why your cabin was so neat."

He chuckled, half turning to face her, leaning a forearm on the rail so that his shoulders were on level with hers. "Now my turn. Tell me something personal about yourself."

"I said you could ask. I didn't say I'd answer."

"Not fair. I've told you my real name, where I come from, where I live, and that I used to kiss a page from a catalog for luck. I've practically given you a credit report. The least you could tell me is what your secret vices are."

Kelsey smiled to herself and finished off the soft drink. It was good, standing there with him in the dark with the gentle sway of the deck beneath her feet. The sound of the water lapping against the hull, the warmth of the night caressing her skin . . . it was comfortable, in an elemental, completely indescribable way.

"Maybe I don't have any," she replied.

"Everybody has a secret vice or two. A hobby they wouldn't like the boss to know about, a little private entertainment . . ."

She looked at him thoughtfully. "You mean like decapitating small animals and keeping their stuffed remains in the basement?"

"Actually I was thinking about playing the horses or watching dirty videotapes, but that will do."

"Somehow I think I already know what your secret vices are."

"We're not talking about me."

Kelsey leaned over to put the empty can in the trash bin. He was partially blocking it with his hip and in order to put the can inside Kelsey had to stretch around him, her breasts brushing against his arm and her pelvis, for an instant, grazing his hip. She knew better than to expect he would move out of her way.

When she straightened up she was smiling, and she gave him a long, measured look. "Sleeping with sailors," she said. "That's my hobby. And my only vice." And she moved away.

Jess waited until her back was fully turned to let his grin break through, and with it, a disbelieving shake of his head. Just when he thought he had her figured out... Not that he would ever be able to completely figure out a woman like that, and not that he even wanted to. But he couldn't recall ever having been surprised as many times in one day as he had been today, with her.

She crossed the deck, glancing for a moment at the lounge chair and sleeping bag he had set out, then she went behind the wheelhouse and returned with another folded chair. The baggy shorts and the shapeless, rumpled T-shirt she wore were about as provocative as a feed sack, and with her hair pinned up in that careless knot of curls she looked like a teenager. Yet still Jess watched her, and enjoyed it.

She set up the chair and settled back in it, propping her feel up on the rail. "God, I wish the sun would rise," she said. Soft impatience underscored her voice. "Nights are such a waste of time."

"Not always. It depends on how you spend them."

He felt, rather than saw, a certain change in her alertness level. Every instinct he possessed warned him not to pursue that, not at this hour, not with her looking so rumpled and wistful, and for once he was determined to listen to his better judgment.

Unfortunately his body had no judgment at all, and he found himself crossing the deck toward her without ever having made up his mind to do so. He sat on the apron that edged the handrail; her bare feet resting on the railing at a level with his shoulder, her bare legs stretching in front of him forever.

He said, "You don't strike me as the dolphin type."

"What is it with you and types? I'm not any type. What's a 'dolphin type,' anyway?"

The slight edge to her voice was a disguise for her discomfiture; Jess recognized it but took no satisfaction from it. He wasn't particularly comfortable at the moment, either, and if he had any sense at all he would have gotten up and moved away. If he lifted his hand only a matter of inches he would be caressing smooth, bare leg, upward over a small, rounded kneecap, then down the slope of her thigh toward her lap. The baggy legs of her shorts were not as concealing as they could have been, and when she sat like this, with her legs propped up, there were tantalizing gaps between flesh and fabric that were difficult to ignore.

He said, "Two types really. The kind that believe they're aliens from Atlantis, sent to save the world, and the kind that *do* want to teach them to retrieve nuclear warheads. You don't fit either profile."

She gave a derisive snort. "Thank you for that, anyway. I'm a biologist, not an animal trainer, and I never even heard your Atlantis theory until just now. I think you're making it up."

He grinned with the sheer delight of the prospect of teasing her, and for a moment almost managed to ignore the closeness of her legs. "You call yourself a woman of the sea? Next you're going to be asking me who King Neptune is and telling me mermaids are really just sea lions in drag."

She smiled. "They are."

It was impossible not to smile at him, impossible not to feel good just looking at him—the lean lines formed by the muscles of his thighs and the dusting of pale hair on his calves and shins; the way the material of his T-shirt was pulled tight across his chest when he leaned back on his elbows against the rail; the way he grinned and the way his eyes lit up with a boyish twinkle when he did . . . he was easy to look at, easy to talk to, easy to be with.

Was he flirting with her? Probably. Just as she was flirting, in her own subtle way, with him. And those were two very excellent reasons why she should go to her cabin this moment and put him firmly out of her mind.

She didn't, of course.

He said, "Why marine biology?"

It was one of those boring cocktail-party questions she hated, but coming from him she somehow didn't mind—perhaps because, at that moment, he lifted his hand in a rather aimless gesture and the backs of his fingers brushed against her foot. What may have started out as an accident ended in a caress that made her stomach tighten in surprise and pleasure.

She answered, "My dad was a human doctor, my mother a vet, so it was pretty much destined I'd go into biology. Living in California, the ocean was my life, so I guess it was only natural."

He hooked his index finger around her small toe, his thumb sweeping lightly over the top of her foot in a gesture that was at once playful and intimate, harmless and subtly erotic. The little prickles of awareness that were generated from his touch traveled all the way to Kelsey's thighs. And his gaze, easy and relaxed, never left hers.

"You could have gone into medicine," he said.

Inane conversation, the kind she usually avoided with a passion. But his fingers moved in a slow caressing stroke around her ankle, and she answered, "Not really. I like fish better than most mammals I know and I certainly prefer sea mammals to human beings any day of the week."

He chuckled. "I can't argue with you there."

The smile was still in his eyes as his hand moved from her ankle upward over her skin. His hands were rough, padded with calluses on the fingertips and heel, his caress warm and firm. Hardness against softness. Masculine roughness against feminine smoothness. Kelsey's throat tightened and her breath felt a little shallow as his fingers moved up to the length of his arm's reach, just above her kneecap, then slowly stroked downward again. And all the time his eyes were watching her, not questioning, not seeking permission, just watching. That look was almost as arousing as his touch.

She said, a little huskily, "I never did finish telling you about the sleeping sharks."

"What's to tell?" His fingers moved upward again, on the inside of her calf. "You said they were harmless."

A light went out somewhere, depriving the deck of even its shadowy, reflected illumination. It seemed the only light that remained in the world was in Jess's eyes.

"Most of the time," she answered. His fingers slipped beneath her knee, stroking the sensitive flesh there. Kelsey could feel the strong muscles of her thighs begin to weaken.

She went on, in a voice as steady as she could make it, "But they're unpredictable. When they're aroused, even sleeping sharks can be dangerous."

He dropped his eyes to her leg for a moment, sweeping its length with his gaze just as he did with his fingers. And then he looked back at her. "So can sleeping with sailors."

"I know."

He drew his hand down the underside of her leg, slowly, lingeringly, as though for the last time. His eyes were clear and sleepy bright. "Sounds like we both should be careful."

Kelsey drew a long, soft breath as his hand encircled her ankle and then briefly, firmly, cupped the arch of her foot. "Yes," she said softly.

She held his eyes steadily as she swung her feet to the deck, and she had every intention then of standing up and going below. She leaned forward to do so, and his hand came beneath her arm, as though to help her to her feet, and then she saw his face, sharply shadowed, and his eyes, passion brilliant, and she could feel her heart beating, slow and hard. She leaned toward him. She tasted him.

It was at first an experimental touch, a clasping and releasing, enacted on impulse and meant to do nothing more than satisfy her curiosity. She wasn't even sure he responded. But in that half second as she hesitated, startled by the sensory shock of the sudden intimacy and unsure whether to back away quickly, or to pursue further, his eyes caught hers.

The hand that once had been assisting her now tightened on her arm, defying her to rise. The other hand was on her knee. He looked at her, studiously, thoughtfully, for what seemed like a very long time, but it could not have been more than a handful of heartbeats. She could see the slow rise and fall of his chest with long, deliberate breaths. His eyes roved from her eyes to her hair, across her forehead and her cheekbones and her nose to her mouth, and his gaze was like a caress; when it reached her mouth her lips parted involuntarily, drawing in a shallow breath. She seemed to sink closer to him, though whether he moved or she did, she couldn't be sure.

His mouth touched hers, just barely, more of a shared breath than a kiss. His tongue traced the shape of her lips with a slow measured sensuality that sent waves of heat through the layers of her skin, suffusing her inner organs. She moved her hands, which had been braced on the sides of her chair, up beneath the sleeves of his T-shirt, and tightened them on his upper arms. She sought his open mouth with her own and he prolonged the play, moving down to caress her jawline with the tip of his tongue, pressing a long, drawing kiss against the pulse in her throat. Her heartbeat was like thunder.

The slight roughness of his chin abraded her cheek as he moved his face over hers. His breath was slow, stirring. With a gentle pressure on her arm he drew her forward, to the very edge of her chair, while the other hand moved upward along her bare leg, his fingers teasing the inside of her thigh. His tongue darted inside her mouth, mating with hers briefly, then away again, sliding over her teeth, the soft flesh of the underside of her lips. She was drowning in dizziness, pulsing heartbeats, waves of heat.

His hands settled on her waist and tightened there. With a firm, sure motion he pulled her out of the chair

and into his arms. At the same moment, on a swift
hungry breath his mouth covered hers; he thrust his
tongue inside.

The flare of sensation was heart stopping, Kelsey
had been kissed before and by experts; she knew the
excitement of first intimacy, the sizzle of chemical reaction, the slow, hot throb of anticipation. She had
never known this blue-white heat before, the meltdown of nerve endings and cell fibers, this sudden
blinding paralysis of awareness. It should have been
just a kiss but it was more than that. It should have
been the ending of a harmless, experimental flirtation; she knew from the first moment it was only the
beginning.

He tasted of nighttime and the sea. His heat filled
her, pushing its way into every pore and synapse,
opening hidden recesses into vivid sensory receptors
that ached with awareness of him. She had not
counted on this. She had not intended this, not for a
moment, not really... And yet her fingers thrust into
his hair, holding him against her as she drank from
him, and it didn't occur to her to stop.

He dragged his mouth away from hers; she felt his
breath, harsh and uneven, on her neck. His voice was
hoarse. "This isn't smart."

"I know." She could hardly form the whisper. His
hands had closed around her breasts, firm and sure,
and the gradually increasing pressure sent a shaft of
weakness down to the pit of her stomach, a blossom-
ing ache between her legs. Her head fell back as his

mouth opened against her throat filling her with heat and pressure and maddening, dizzying pleasure.

"Jess," she gasped.

"What?" Husky, barely audible. His mouth moved down, covering the place where his hands had been, and she forgot what it was she wanted to say.

Her hands pushed beneath his T-shirt, over his rib cage and upward across his chest. She had been wrong about his chest; it was covered with a fine pattern of smooth, silky hair, distinctly defining the arch of his breast muscles then narrowing into a center line. She traced that center pattern downward until it disappeared inside his shorts, and she felt his sharp catch of breath as she slipped her fingers inside his waistband. She had been right. He wore nothing underneath.

His hands came up, holding her face. She could feel his breath across her damp, heated skin, and his eyes were intensely dark, brilliantly lit. He might have said her name, she could not hear over the roaring of a thousand oceans in her ears. Dimly Kelsey knew that it shouldn't be like this, she had not meant for it to be like this, but they both had passed the moment for indecision or regrets long ago. Even if she had wanted to she couldn't have turned back. And she didn't want to.

His hand moved below his waist and she heard the rustle of clothing being rearranged as his arm slipped around her shoulder, lowering her to the deck. Her heart was pounding, the night air tantalized her bare skin when her shorts were pushed aside; his flesh was hot against hers. His breath, her breath, tongues tasting and skipping and dancing across each other...and his eyes, always his eyes, boring into her soul. Her hands were on his back, fingers tightening, her legs surrounding him, and he was against her, pushing himself inside in a sweet, powerful invasion that robbed her breath and stripped her senses and left her helpless against the urgency her own body demanded of her.

It was too swift, too powerful, too intense; an explosion of sensations, one upon the other, that afterward she had difficulty even remembering, much less cataloging. She arched to meet him as his mouth covered hers; he thrust deeper and her fingers dug into his shoulders. Her cry of rapture was lost inside his mouth as almost immediately the waves of pleasure began to gather inside her and to escalate, concentric circles like ripples on a pond, spreading wider and wider, erupting into shudders of blinding, cascading pleasure that seemed to go on forever. His hands went beneath her and he clasped her to him, hard, with the power of his own release. Then they collapsed against each other, damp faces pressed together, breaths intermingled, limbs still weakly interwined. They were stunned, exhausted and shaken, together and separately, to their very souls.

After a long time of thundering heartbeats and spinning stars—an hour, a night, a lifetime—Jess reluctantly eased himself away from her. But he captured her hand and threaded his fingers through hers, holding it lightly, weakly against his chest. He was almost afraid to look at her for what he might find in her face. He hadn't expected this to happen. God knew he hadn't planned on it. And if he had, he would have never, in his wildest fantasy expected it to be like this.... He wanted to say something. He didn't know what to say.

Kelsey looked at him in the dark. His profile turned toward her, his eyes upon the sky, his lips parted for breath and his hair, wet with exertion and clinging to his scalp...his hand holding hers. She could feel his chest jerk with the hammer beat of his heart, a counterpoint to the gradually slowing weight that pounded against her own rib cage. He was beautiful to her, just as he had been the first moment she saw him, when she could not have guessed how vastly the reality would surpass the fantasy.

And it wasn't a fantasy. The recognition struck her with a little chill that started in the pit of her stomach and gradually worked its way outward, and she wasn't sure whether it was a shiver of wonder or horror that finally prickled her skin. She suspected it was a little of both. A harmless flirtation, an innocent fantasy... Jess Seward was neither anymore. He was the only man in twenty-eight years who had ever been able to make her forget herself, lose control, override her best judgment. Their coming together had been like a tidal wave, sweeping away everything in its path, impossible to stop. She couldn't ignore what they had just shared, nor could she forget it—any more than she could forget the man. He was very real, very solid, and he was not going to go away.

She wondered what he was thinking. She didn't even know what she was thinking. She should say something, do something. She couldn't move.

And then Jess turned to her. She could see only the glow of his eyes in the dark, but his voice sounded hesitant, uncertain, "Kelsey . . ."

She stiffened, pulling her hand away. "Get dressed!" she hissed, and sat up quickly.

He sat up, staring at her.

"Hurry, damn it!" She was already pulling on her shorts.

And then he heard it—footsteps on the dock, the sound of low voices. By the time Craig and Dean boarded, moving carefully so as not to awake their supposed sleeping colleague, Jess was dressed and Kelsey was moving toward the wheelhouse. He caught her arm.

She cast him an impatient look.

"Kelsey—"

Behind him one of the other men called softly, "Hey, Kelsey, is that you? You awake?"

Kelsey pulled her arm away, and Jess looked over his shoulder. "Never mind," he muttered.

But it didn't matter. She was gone.

Five

Jess hated mornings-after. He never knew what was expected of him, he never knew how to behave, and even after thirty-one years of observation and experience in the human condition—a good fifteen of which, easily, had been devoted to the baffling subject of the interaction between the sexes—he was never quite sure what a night like the one he and Kelsey Morgan had shared was supposed to mean.

Not what it meant to him—that was a subject he wouldn't be able to tackle for a long time yet—but what it meant to her. Was she embarrassed, shocked, angry? Did she expect intimacy now, some kind of commitment, a continuation of this new level in their relationship—or did she just want to forget it had ever happened?

It bothered Jess, more than it should have, to consider that she might just want to forget it. Forget him.

She had appeared on deck at dawn, just as he was preparing to cast off, but she hadn't even glanced in his direction. She was busy giving orders to the other two, and Jess supposed he should have been grateful for that, but he wasn't. In fact, he resented the presence of Craig and Dean to a ridiculous degree. If they had not appeared unexpectedly last night, Jess might have had a chance to have some of his questions answered. Now they were keeping Kelsey away from him, and he further resented the fact that they both looked so calm and well rested when he hadn't closed his eyes all night.

It would be easier, of course, to simply forget it. He had enough trouble dealing with the morning-after with ordinary women, but with Kelsey...what could he say to her? That he hadn't intended it to happen, that he usually had much more self-control, that believe it or not, he hadn't done anything that reckless and impulsive since he was eighteen years old. That it scared the hell out of him because with her, for that moment frozen in time when the world had shifted on its axis and reason and restraint spun out of reach, something inside him had been subtly but fundamentally changed. He didn't know how to explain it and he didn't know how to define it, but last night was not something he could simply forget. That was why he didn't know what to say to her.

He watched her moving around the deck in the soft fuzzy gray light of early morning and watching her made his throat dry up and his heart beat faster—not because she was sexy as hell, which she was, and not because just looking at her brought back memories so sharp and poignant they were almost physical, which it did, but because she was Kelsey. She fascinated him and mystified him and frightened him, just a little, and when he thought about the two of them last night he couldn't believe it had really happened...and then he couldn't believe it hadn't been happening forever, that was how right it felt, how magical and sure. And *that* was frightening.

Generally this hour of the morning was his favorite time of day—soft and colorless, like an imagination that wasn't quite awake yet, tasting of night's leftovers and the day's promises. Moving into the channel, the breeze was just strong enough to feel cool and the sea was calm, the engines thrummed like a kitten's purr, and generally he would have savored a moment like this. But there was Kelsey, in white shorts and tan legs, thighs so lean and smooth they could have belonged to a department store mannequin, stomach flat between the slight rise of her hipbones, perfect knees, slim calves... She was wearing a full-cut white poplin jacket with the sleeves pushed up, and it billowed in the breeze, hiding the rest of her figure from him. She had caught back her hair in a thick, coarse braid, but it was still curly and wild on top. Her feet were encased in scuffed white deck shoes, and even her feet looked beautiful to him. He wondered if she had suffered the same sleepless night he had, but he didn't know her well enough to tell. He knew her, in fact, hardly at all.

The scientists had set up a small worktable on deck, and she was standing there now, leaning over Dean's shoulder as they studied some papers, gesturing with her coffee cup. When Jess least expected it, she glanced up and looked straight at him. Then she said something else to Dean, and came into the wheelhouse.

Jess said, "Good morning."

Kelsey reached for the charts, but didn't respond. Somehow, even a returned "Good morning" seemed risky to her, laden with implications she didn't want him to read and suggestions she didn't want to make.

She felt stupid, awkward, and angry with herself for feeling either. How could she be in charge of this expedition when she couldn't even stay in charge of her emotions? She had been avoiding him all morning and she was sure he had noticed; that made her angry, too. But she didn't know what to say to him. Every time she looked at him a wave of heated, breath-robbing memories went through her; her stomach grew tight and her legs went weak and her mind was, for the space of several seconds, as blank as a freshly washed blackboard; she couldn't think, much less speak. All she could do was feel, and what she felt was too complex for analysis. She knew, because she had spent all night trying to analyze it, listening to her heart pound, reliving his touch and his taste and trying, with all her might, to make sense of what had happened, or failing that, to at least put it out of her mind . . . and succeeding at neither.

She knew she couldn't avoid him forever, which was why she had forced herself to come into the wheelhouse. It was a morning like any other, and there was work to be done. She could handle this. She had to.

She even made herself move close to him, glancing at the loran and compass over his shoulder, then turned back to the charts. He smelled like night wind and the sea.

"How much longer in the channel?" she asked without glancing up.

His voice was as impersonal as hers, though perfectly pleasant. "Another ten minutes."

Kelsey wondered what he was thinking. What *did* men think at a time like this? Did they think anything at all? And if they did would any woman ever know what it was?

She quickly brought her attention back to the business at hand and tapped the chart perfunctorily. "Cut the engines right about here, will you? We want to take some readings."

He glanced over to see the area she indicated. "Sure thing. Any of that coffee left?"

She refolded the charts. Her heart started beating a little faster. Why should a casual question about coffee do that? Except that it wasn't the question. It was that he had looked at her, full on, for the first time since she had come into the wheelhouse. "In the galley," she replied.

"Seeing as how this isn't a real good time for me to leave my post, some people might think it an act of kindness to bring me a cup."

Even such an offhand comment seemed far too personal to her, an invitation toward intimacy or companionability or even conversation, and she didn't know how to react. She didn't know what he expected of her. *Damn* she hated this.

She replied shortly, "You wanted to drive."

He looked at her. "Kelsey..."

Panic assailed her with that look, with the sudden gentleness that couched the single word. "If the rest of that sentence has the words 'about last night' in it," she interrupted briskly, "I don't want to hear it." She returned the charts to their position and started to leave.

Jess almost let her go. In fact, for about two seconds it seemed the only sensible thing to do and he thanked his lucky stars that she had made it so easy. And then the shock wore off and, without even pausing to look over his shoulder at her his hand shot out and caught her arm.

She resisted angrily and he pulled harder—perhaps too hard, because she stumbled and bumped her hip against the work shelf.

Kelsey rubbed her arm when he released it, and glared at him. Adrenaline was pumping, and she knew it was as much from a good, healthy surge of perfectly justifiable anger as it was from his touch, his closeness, and the sight of him, strong and tall and in control as he stood at the helm.

"Is that what you wanted to know?" she demanded. "That you can win a tug-of-war?"

"With one hand tied behind my back," he pointed out.

His tone was mild but his jaw was hard. He stood in profile to her, his eyes straight ahead, his hand resting with casual competence on the wheel, one foot propped up against the lower panel of the instrument station. The first rays of the early sun broke through the cloud cover and painted the planes of his face golden, sparkling in his hair. Just looking at him made Kelsey's throat hurt, and the fact shocked her. She jerked her eyes away.

"Congratulations," she said. "I'll issue the bulletin." She turned toward the door again.

Jess's hand tightened on the wheel and he could feel the muscles in his shoulders starting to knot. But with what he considered a heroic demonstration of self-control he replied mildly, "Go ahead. I can tell you're busy. I'll just moor the boat right here and wait until you have time to talk."

She stopped, turning stiffly. Jess was glad he couldn't see her face because her voice was like ice. "What?" she demanded tightly.

Jess kept his tone conversational and his eyes on his work. "I have something to say. It may or may not be about last night. It'd only be good manners of you to listen."

Kelsey stood just inside the door, poised for flight. Her heart was pounding and her skin felt hot, but inside she was clammy with dread. This wasn't like her, not at all. She wasn't afraid of confrontation. She wasn't afraid of anything. Yet she felt as though he was backing her into a corner and all she wanted to do was to get away from him, to never have to meet his eyes again...

She said, "I've never been accused of having good manners."

"That I can believe."

And she couldn't stand it anymore. She couldn't keep wondering what he was thinking, dreading to find out, letting him hold her captive to the suspense and her own uncertainty. "Look," she said abruptly. "Let's not make a big deal about this okay? Last night..." She lowered her voice just a fraction, not wanting to be overheard. "It happened, it's over. I think it's best if we both just forget it."

Jess's voice, in return, was matter-of-fact, but she could see the tight ridges of his knuckles as he gripped the wheel, making a course correction as they approached a harbor buoy.

"Yeah, I figured you'd say that. It'd be kind of hard giving orders to somebody you've slept with, wouldn't it? So the easiest thing to do would be to just pretend it didn't happen."

She could feel hostility crackling behind the words like static electricity, and the sparks that were cast off only ignited her own defensive anger. Kelsey drew herself up and responded coolly, "That's right. Are you finished?"

"Just one more question." He eased back on the throttle, adjusting the speed to the turn. "Is this your usual rotten disposition, or are you trying to make a point?''

''Both.'' With every word that was exchanged the tension between them wound a little tighter, like the mainspring on a watch; another turn or two and something was going to break. Kelsey knew that, but she still couldn't keep the rancor out of her voice as she went on, ''Look, we're stuck together for two weeks, whether we like it or not. If you think I'm going to spend the next fourteen days trying to remember to smile every time you walk by and call you 'darling' and tell you how wonderful you are just because we—''

''And I'm not going to spend the next two weeks tiptoeing around on my own ship,'' he interrupted harshly, ''trying to stay out of your way, feeling like I've committed some kind of crime. I wasn't exactly alone out there last night, you know, and come to think of it wasn't entirely *my* idea—''

''Is that it?'' she cried incredulously. ''Is that what's been festering inside your tiny little brain? That *I* seduced you?''

''I didn't say that!''

''What the hell *are* you saying, then?''

He turned on her. His eyes were as dark as thunderheads and his jawline was tight; frustration and anger radiated from him with a force that practically crackled in the air. ''What do you want from me, lady?'' he demanded.

Kelsey drew in her breath sharply, and she wasn't sure whether the little stab of unexpected sensation in the pit of her stomach was from renewed anger, or from the sudden, unexpected tug of desire. She turned his words back on him. "What do you want from *me?* Because if you think last night changes anything between us—"

"There isn't anything between us!"

"That's right, and we're going to keep it that way. That's what I want from you!"

It *was* what she wanted. She was certain of it. Except that when he looked at her, long and steadily, with eyes that were cloudy and bitter and, far back in their depths, perhaps concealing just the smallest shadow of hurt, she didn't want that at all, and she didn't want him to want it...and it was crazy; she was crazy for even considering such a thing. There was nothing between them and there could never be anything between them and that was the way she wanted it.

Jess's lips tightened, and he jerked his eyes away, looking straight ahead. "Fine," he said.

"Fine," she repeated, just as forcefully. She realized then that her nails were digging into her palms, and she made herself unclench her fists.

She turned to go, and this time he didn't try to stop her. Hurt and anger and a strange, poignant-tasting disappointment thickened the air between them. Kelsey hadn't expected that; she hadn't expected any of this. He was making her act like a thirteen-year-old, and she hated it. She hated the sound of her own spiteful words and she hated the anger that stiffened his shoulders and she hated the fact that she didn't know how it had happened. He hadn't been angry when she came in. *She* hadn't been angry when she came in. What was the matter with her?

She stopped, bracing her hand against the doorframe, and took a slow, deep breath. This could not go on for two weeks. She couldn't let it go on for another two minutes. With an effort, she turned around to face him. "Look," she said carefully, "I can deal with this. Can you?"

The engine powered down, settling into a smooth, steady hum that throbbed beneath Kelsey's feet. Jess swiveled the captain's chair around until he was looking at her, and he looked at her for a long time. His expression was unreadable.

He said, "Yeah. I think so."

She cleared her throat. "It'll be a lot easier if you keep on acting like an idiot. Keep reminding me why I don't like you."

A spark of amusement softened the gravity of his gaze, resulting in an absurd little leap of pleasure for Kelsey.

"Yeah. Same to you."

She made her neck muscles relax, and even tried to smile, but she couldn't quite manage it. She glanced away. Her voice was stiffer than it should have been as she added, "We're both adults. These things happen."

She knew that was not what she meant to say even before she saw the wry tightening of his lips. "All the time."

She lifted her chin, refusing to let the heat that stung her cheeks defeat her. He was obviously not going to make it any easier for her, but that was all right. She was used to doing difficult things by herself.

She went on, "I'm sorry if I was short with you earlier. This isn't— I'm not very good at this sort of thing."

He said quietly, "Believe it or not, neither am I."

She looked at him sharply, but saw no signs of sarcasm on his face. In fact he looked a little wary of her, and beneath that, almost apologetic.

And he still had the most beautiful eyes she had ever seen.

She felt her shoulders relax a fraction and her voice felt a little easier as she said, "It's just that—I told you before how important this trip is to me. I can't afford to be distracted by—"

He broke in firmly, "Look. Think about this for a minute. I run a charter business. Three-quarters of all the runs I make involve at least one beautiful woman. If I made it a habit to sleep with every one of them I wouldn't have time to steer the boat so I have a policy—I don't mix business and pleasure. Last night was the first time I've ever broken that rule and I'm just as embarrassed about it as you are. And if you think for one minute I'm going to let it happen again, I wish you'd give me a little credit. The fact of the matter is, I've got more to lose than you do."

She stared at him, and she didn't know for a moment whether to be insulted or grateful. What she felt was a slow, reluctant admiration, and after a moment that emotion made itself known in the resigned smile that tugged at her lips. "Yeah," she said. "I guess so."

And she was thinking about what he'd said. *Embarrassed.* Was that what it was, then? Was that the peculiar hot-and-cold sensation that went through her whenever she looked at him? Was that what addled her brain and shortened her temper and made her say such stupid things? Last night she had lost control of her emotions, she had let her will be swept away, she had immersed herself in a fantasy and forgotten who she was and what she valued; she had shared the most intimate of human acts with a virtual stranger, and that was certainly reason enough to be embarrassed.

Even now, looking at him, the sensations swept over her again—his skin, hot against hers, his muscles hard and tight, his breath and his touch and his simple power...the wave of remembrance began in her stomach and flooded upward to her hairline, tingling in her fingertips and aching in her calves. Was that embarrassment? She did not think so.

She wasn't embarrassed about having made love to him. She was embarrassed about having run away afterward.

She met his eyes then, and it was almost as though he read her thoughts. It was a rare moment of understanding that wouldn't ordinarily happen even between real lovers, which they certainly weren't, but in that moment the pretense was wiped away and there was, quite simply, nothing to be embarrassed about.

The last of the tension drained from her shoulders and she said, "I don't guess we can pretend it didn't happen."

His smile was soft and a little absent, and it made Kelsey's breath catch. It was exactly the kind of smile a woman wanted to see on the face of a man when he remembered having made love to her.

He agreed, "No."

Her eyes were on his arm, which was crooked casually over the back of his chair: tanned and sinewy, dusted with golden hairs . . . she had never found out whether he had a tattoo on his shoulder.

She forced her eyes back to his face and continued determinedly, "But that doesn't mean it's going to happen again."

"Absolutely."

She thought he was agreeing with her; from the gentle play of lights in his eyes it was impossible to tell. In fact, lost for a moment in those eyes, it was impossible to remember exactly what she had wanted him to agree to.

And that was when she caught herself on the edge of the danger zone, and pulled back abruptly. She turned for the door, making her voice as casually impersonal as she knew how as she said, "Give me about a ten-minute warning before we hit those coordinates, okay?"

He turned back to the controls. "Right."

But there was one more thing. She stopped at the door, knowing that if she left without saying it she would hate herself, but hating herself even more for the necessity of saying it.

"Listen." She drew a breath, but couldn't make herself turn to face him. She heard the faint squeak of his chair as he swiveled to look at her, she could feel his eyes on her back as though his gaze were a touch.

She finished, so quietly the words were almost swallowed by the engines, "It's not my hobby."

He was silent for so long she thought he hadn't heard, or didn't care. She took a step across the threshold, stiff with humiliation.

And then he said, with a kind of incredulous amusement and so gently that it made her breath catch, "I know that."

Kelsey would have given a great deal to see the expression on his face then, but every instinct she possessed warned her that could be a big mistake. She left quickly, and without looking back.

"Of course there's never really been an effective shark suit," Craig was explaining earnestly. "They either don't work at all, or they're too cumbersome to be practical, and they're always going to leave some part of the body exposed. And until now they've failed to perform one vital function—which is to prevent attack in the first place. I mean it's certainly desirable to escape serious injury during an attack, but when one is engaged in delicate underwater work the ideal would be not to have to deal with an attack at all, don't you agree?"

Jess nodded and tried to look interested. That wouldn't have been so difficult under ordinary circumstances—Craig might not be the most compelling speaker in the world, but his subject was intriguing—but it was hard for Jess to keep his mind on anything when his eyes kept straying to Kelsey.

They were moored some five miles off the coast, taking their evening meal on deck while the last rays of the sun spread a panorama of indigo and orange across the sky. Fresh fruit, cold cuts and bakery bread provided the first night's fare; as time wore on, canned staples and freeze-dried meats would compose most of their meals. Traditionally on all Jess's charters, the captain provided wine on the first night, and the chablis, sipped from plastic cups, added a festive touch. In fact, everything about the meal seemed festive to Jess and had started to seem so the minute Kelsey had sat down in the chair across from him.

He was starting to feel like an oversexed teenager who couldn't keep his eyes off the only woman on board, but the truth was, it was hard *not* to look at her. And it had nothing at all to do with sex—or at least not much. She had the kind of presence that demanded attention, whether she was eating a ham sandwich or frowning over a computer printout or shouting navigational commands against the wind—a man simply had to look at her, if for no other reason than to make sure he was always prepared for what she might do next.

What she was doing now was sharing a rather rueful smile with Dean over something Craig had said.

One bare arm was hooked over the back of her chair, the other elbow was propped on the table, her fingers holding the cup of wine loosely around the rim. Jess found his eyes drawn to the place where the tank top she wore separated the curve of her shoulder from the curve of her breast, and the slimmest semicircle of whiter flesh just inside the armhole of her top. When he moved his eyes upward again she was looking at him, and reluctantly he turned his attention back to Craig.

"So this invention of yours," he said, "it solves all those problems?"

Craig nodded enthusiastically. "We've known for a long time, you see, that the most powerful stimulus to a shark is electronic fields—"

With a little grimace of impatience, Kelsey rose. "Excuse me, gentlemen, but I've heard all this before. Dean, don't forget you drew KP tonight."

Dean started building himself another sandwich. "Yeah, well, I don't understand why it is that whenever we draw straws you never end up with the short one."

"That's because I cut the straws," she tossed over her shoulder.

Jess tried not to watch her as she walked away.

Craig, hardly able to contain his enthusiasm over an untried—and practically captive—audience, went on, "As I was saying, that's why a shark will attack a boat it can't eat, or a shark cage instead of the diver swimming just outside—it always goes for the biggest electromagnetic field. The solution, of course, is to find a way to mask the body's electronic field—"

"See," Dean said around a mouthful of ham and cheese, "that's where I've got to argue with you. First place, nobody has ever proven that the shark's receptivity to electrical stimuli is as important as you say it is. In the second place, you can't overlook the fact—"

"Now wait just a minute. You've seen the results of my studies—"

"Yeah, and they were impressive, as far as they went. The thing I'm saying is . . ."

Jess waited until the two of them were so deeply immersed in debate they didn't even notice when he emptied the last of the wine into his glass, then he quietly got up and walked away.

It wasn't that he went deliberately in search of Kelsey. If she hadn't been readily available he wouldn't have combed every nook and cranny for her. On the other hand, it was a safe bet that on a boat that size she wouldn't have gone very far, and it certainly wasn't Jess's intention to avoid her . . . although, perhaps a more sensible man might have done so.

The storage lockers on the starboard side behind the wheelhouse were topped with waterproof cushions and doubled as extra seating space. She was sitting with her back leaning against the rail, one slim leg drawn up and her arm resting across her knee, watching the sky and the sea. She didn't acknowledge his presence, but neither did she leave when she saw him. He sat down beside her.

Claim your FREE books and gifts here

Yes Please send me three books and two gifts absolutely FREE. Please also reserve a special Reader Service subscription for me. If I decide to subscribe, I will receive two each of the very latest titles from the Mills & Boon Temptation, Silhouette Special Edition and Desire series every month. Six books for £10.20 postage and packing FREE, thats just £1.70 per book. If I decide not to subscribe I shall write to you within 10 days. The FREE books and gifts remain mine to keep in any case. I understand that I am under no obligation whatsoever. I may cancel or suspend my subscription at any time simply by writing to you. I am over 18 years of age.

8S2X

Ms/Mrs/Miss/Mr _____

Address _____

_____

_____

_____ Postcode _____

"I take it you don't think much of your friend's shark suit."

His voice was casual and so was his manner, and Kelsey tried to match it. There was no reason for them to try to spend the rest of the voyage trying to avoid each other or being awkward around each other; she was glad he had taken the initiative in surmounting that barrier. The least she could do was meet him halfway.

"Let's just say it's highly experimental," she answered with a lift of her shoulders. "Craig is really a brilliant man and he's got the theory down pat, but in practice it just doesn't work—at least it hasn't in the lab."

The lockers were more than six feet long; there was plenty of room on either side of her for another person to sit, or even stretch out, comfortably. But Jess had chosen to sit so close to her that his hip brushed hers and his arm, propped up on the rail radiated its warmth into the muscles of her shoulder. Kelsey, who had always been defensive of her personal space, wondered whether he did it on purpose, as a form of intimidation. And of course she wouldn't move away.

He said quietly, "Look."

He lifted his glass in a gesture toward the horizon and Kelsey followed his gaze. No further comment or acknowledgement was necessary from one sea lover to another; words would have stripped the moment of its magic and diminished the spectacle by limiting it to what only words could describe. As the sun balanced itself on the horizon line it formed a perfect circle, bi-

sected by the dark line of sea and sky, reflected below
and blazing gold above. As they watched, the night
stretched tenebrous fingers across the face of the sun,
deep purple, dark navy, ink black. The drama was reflected on the face of the sea as though captured by a
giant mirror, each color and change enhanced and
played back upon itself. And then, as though blown
out with a breath, the light was gone. Shadow colors
glowed in the sky where the sun once had been, and
twilight, lavender and gray, settled its soft folds
around the two on the deck.

Kelsey looked at him, and she could count on the
fingers of one hand the moments in her life that had
been more perfect than this. She smiled, and he smiled
back. They didn't say anything. That was the best
part: neither one of them felt they had to talk.

And yet there was so much that needed to be said.

It surprised Kelsey that he was the one to begin. As
the shadows deepened and the breeze drew away the
heat of the day, they sipped their wine and listened to
the sound of the sea. His tone was easy when he spoke,
as though he were picking up the threads of a conversation that had been only recently interrupted.

"The thing is," he said, "I don't want you to take
this personally, but I have really rotten luck with relationships. I've never been with any woman for more
than a week who didn't end up hating me." And he
shrugged. "I've never been able to figure out why that
is. Personally I think I'm a hell of a nice guy."

She grinned, too startled and amused to dissemble.
"Yeah, you and me, too."

"You think I'm a hell of a nice guy?"

"No, I think I am. Too nice to have a voodoo doll named after me, which rumor has it is what the last guy I went out with did."

He chuckled. "No offense, but somehow that doesn't surprise me."

She sipped her wine. "Thanks a lot."

It was her turn, and the words were not as difficult as she had expected. She gazed into the distance, and she said, "All my life, I've been good at things. School, sports, writing papers, making speeches, even fund-raising... give me a problem to solve or a theory to prove or a job to do or a lesson to learn and it's done, no problem. Things like that are easy for me. But I have really rotten judgment about people. I don't understand them, I don't relate to them, and I never seem to do the right thing. I rub people the wrong way. I don't know why. I expect all the wrong things, I look for all the wrong things, and I end up *doing* all the wrong things. My dad says I'm too impatient to be bogged down by the human race. I had a boyfriend once—we even lived together for a while—who said I just wasn't interested enough to hold on to a relationship." She shrugged and glanced at her nearly empty glass. "Maybe he was right. Because it's not just men, but people in general—I never seem to be paying attention when it counts."

She ventured a glance at him, and was both relieved and a little surprised by the interested, thoughtful expression on his face. No, it was more than just interest. It was understanding.

She said, "Anyway, I don't know why I told you all that, except that—well, I wanted you to know it's nothing personal. I'm just really not interested."

His lips curved at one corner, and he gave a small shake of his head. "We're quite a pair, huh?"

He looked at her in the gray-blue evening light, his eyes brimming with repressed amusement, and affected a sober tone as he said, "So, Kelsey, how come a nice guy like you never got married?"

The slow grin that crossed her face seemed to spread from the inside out; she felt easy and content for the first time that day. "I don't know," she replied. "Holding out for a hero, I guess."

He shared her grin. "Lucky me. That's one thing I'll never be."

She chuckled, and so did he. When her laughter faded she was leaning back against the rail, resting on his outstretched arm, and his fingers were absently toying with one of her curls. And though the laughter was gone the camaraderie was not, and she did not sit up, or move her head.

She said, "You're not doing a very good job of reminding me how much I dislike you."

"Neither are you."

She glanced up at him, trying not to linger too long on the shadowed angle of his jaw, or the strong line of his neck, or to remember how his flesh had tasted, last night, against her tongue. She said, "On the other hand, the more I get to know you, the less I'll probably like you."

"The story of my life."

She could feel his eyes on her; eyes that didn't just observe, but touched. His hip and his thigh formed an intimate line of warmth against hers, a joining seam. It was hard not to look at him, hard not to remember, hard not to react when simply being near him made her feel charged with awareness.

"I mean," she continued firmly, "what happened was really stupid. And I generally don't do stupid things."

"Yeah, me, either." He sipped from his glass, moving his eyes out over the sea. "I don't guess this is a good time to tell you that it was also the most incredible thing that's ever happened to me."

She swallowed hard. "No. It's not."

He didn't look at her, and his voice was matter-of-fact. "Not just fireworks. Armageddon."

"Nuclear meltdown."

He glanced at her. "Right."

She smiled. She couldn't help it. "Right."

He smiled back.

After a moment she dropped her eyes to her own glass. Her fingers tightened a little on the plastic. "It really *was* stupid," she repeated, a little huskily. "And it *is* over. But..." And she glanced up at him. "I'm not sorry."

His gaze was steady and softly lit, as though with invisible starlight. "Yeah," he agreed. "Me, either."

Kelsey thought she admired him more in that brief moment than she had ever admired anyone—for being honest, for being understanding, and for being still when he surely must have known that all it would have taken was a touch, the smallest of movements, the breath of a kiss and she would have been in his arms again. Because she was remembering, and he was remembering, and the awareness between them was like heat lightning, silent and pulsing.

She stood abruptly. "Well. I've still got work to do."

"Did you guys run a check on your dive gear?"

"Dean's doing that tonight."

"I'll give him a hand."

"Thanks." She hesitated, but couldn't think of anything else to say. She walked away.

A few steps across the deck she thought of something, and turned back. "Hey, sailor," she called softly, and a little reluctantly. "For an amateur, you did okay today."

His chuckle, drifting through the warm night, was her only reply.

She walked toward the bow.

"Hey, Legs."

She turned, a little startled, and peered toward his silhouette, still lounging back against the rail.

"So did you."

She continued on her way, grinning to herself in the dark.

Six

A tourist, having decided the Falpor Islands might make a nice vacation spot, would be sadly disappointed when he arrived. Not only were there no hotels, swimming pools or golf courses, there were—as far as the naked eye could see—no islands. The Falpors were, in fact, less of a land mass than an oceanographic location; the two miles of caves, cliffs and uneven underwater terrain suggested to some oceanographers a small group of sunken islands but, to all intents and purposes, it was just another area of ocean. The ocean floor ranged from a shallow of fifteen feet—which had proven a hazard to ocean-going vessels before the area had been definitively charted—to a depth of over two hundred. The wide variety of temperatures, depths and terrain provided a virtual haven for all kinds of marine wildlife, and for the biologists who studied it.

Unfortunately the appeal of the Falpors was not limited to scientists. Treasure hunters were lured by the shipwrecks caused by the shallows, sports divers by the natural beauty, and fishermen by the abundance of easy catches. Though the relative obscurity and the difficulty of reaching the islands had protected them from all but the fishermen for years, the recent intrusion by man had begun to seriously threaten the ecosystem that had attracted men to the area in the first place. Aggressive lobbying by environmentalists had brought the region under partial governmental protection—requiring sportsmen and treasure hunters to file for special permits before entering the area—but a great deal more remained to be done. If Kelsey's work in the region turned out as she planned, the cause of turning the Falpors into a totally protected area would be advanced another step.

Two nautical miles before reaching their technical destination, Kelsey ordered—though Jess preferred to think of it as a request—a crisscross approach. Dean and Craig stationed themselves inside the wheelhouse with Jess, Craig monitoring the echo sounder, which identified schools of fish as the boat passed over, and Dean keeping an eye on the sonar and an ear on the radio transmitter. It did not take a genius to catch on to the search-pattern grid they needed, but Kelsey was in and out of the wheelhouse constantly, peering over Jess's shoulder, making minute course corrections, doing everything but physically taking the wheel from his hand. Finally Jess put on his stereo headphones so he didn't have to listen to her, he stopped looking at her when she came inside, and after a time she left him alone.

The day was thick with murky clouds, but they had left the worst of the coastal heat behind. The sea was steel gray and as smooth as silk, the kind of sea that troubled sailors and delighted fishermen. Jess, who didn't have to depend on a capricious wind for his destination or a fisherman's net for his living, could appreciate the moody day for just what it was—cool and mysterious, and as fascinating as the woman of whom it reminded him.

That woman had stationed herself on the flying bridge with a pair of binoculars, and had not been back down to the wheelhouse in almost twenty minutes. It amazed Jess dimly that her attention span was that long; there was nothing to be seen except a lone fishing boat perhaps a half-mile distance, which until now had been following a search-pattern roughly parallel to theirs.

Apparently the fishing boat had had more luck than the scientists in locating a school. Jess watched absently as it began to pay out its net, pulling off his headphones as the tape came to an end. "I wonder what she's looking for up there," he commented, glancing upward toward the flying bridge. It stood to reason that Kelsey could not be expected to spot anything in the water, even with her binoculars, that the electronic equipment wouldn't pick up first. Not that

Jess was complaining—he would much rather have her on the bridge than down here—but he was curious.

He hadn't really expected an answer, and was surprised when Dean turned around. An expression of dread crossed the younger man's face and the matchstick he had been chewing dropped from his mouth. He seemed to be sharing Jess's view of the fishing boat.

"Oh, no." It was a half groan. "Oh, man. I wish you hadn't asked that."

Jess heard the footsteps storming down the ladder only seconds before Kelsey burst into the wheelhouse. "Pull up alongside," she commanded.

He stared at her. "What?"

She jerked the binoculars off her neck and thrust them to him. Her lips were tight and her eyes were blazing and there were two spots of wild color on her face, which was otherwise terrifyingly still. He should have known better than to take his eyes off her, looking the way she did, but he had an excuse in that she caught him completely off guard.

He took the binoculars and swung them toward the fishing boat. But he barely had time to make out the call name of the other vessel before Kelsey pushed past him and he heard the engines start to power up. He spun around, grabbing her arm, but she wouldn't budge from the controls.

"What do you think you're doing?"

"I'm cutting across his bow," Kelsey replied grimly. She eased forward on the throttle and made a thirty-degree starboard turn.

"Are you crazy?" Jess shouted at her. "We're going to rip through their nets!"

She said lowly, "Good," and pushed the throttle into greater speed.

Dean muttered, "Oh, man. Oh, man, I knew this trip was going too smooth." And he left the wheelhouse.

Craig said, "Nothing on sonar."

And Jess wasted a good three seconds in utter astonishment, staring at her, before he regained control of his senses and grabbed the radio microphone. "*Sea Wizard* this is the *Miss Santa Fe*. We are coming across your bow. Do not pay out your net! Repeat, do not pay out your net!"

Then he tossed the microphone down and grabbed Kelsey's shoulders with every intention of flinging her across the room and with just enough fury to do it without a twinge of guilt. But just then he realized what maneuver she was attempting and every muscle in his body froze, like gears seizing up in an overworked machine. Only his fingers continued to tighten on her shoulder, and tighten, until—if he had given it any thought at all—he might have expected her bones to crumble into powder between his fingertips. But she was so intent she did not even notice.

The fishing boat was using a purse seine—a huge net that was anchored with floats around the boat and weights on the bottom, and could be drawn up at the top like a purse when it was filled with fish. Depending upon the size of the school of fish it had targeted the net could spread out as much as fifteen-hundred feet in diameter, dwarfing the boat that controlled it. Jess's practiced eye told him that this net was probably no more than five hundred feet across and almost half of it—from stern to midships—had been payed out. Even if they had heard Jess's warning call, they could not have pulled in the net in time, and chances were they had not heard, or paid attention if they had.

They were paying attention now. When Kelsey had first throttled up she had marked a direct course at full speed for the *Sea Wizard,* almost as though she planned to broadside it. At that course and speed there was no way she could avoid running over the net, a fact that the men on board the other boat were just beginning to recognize. They were so close that Jess could see the angry faces of the fisherman who were shouting and waving their arms; he could almost hear the profanity they yelled over the sound of the engines. And when they were within a matter of feet— when the net floats were bobbing before the *Miss Santa Fe* so close that a man could have leaned over the rail and grabbed one of them—Kelsey suddenly throttled down, cut across her own wake and neatly, unbelievably, skirted the net and slid toward the bow.

Cold beads of perspiration were standing on Jess's forehead when Kelsey flipped on the audio speaker and snatched up the microphone. "Attention, *Sea Wizard!*" Her voice boomed over sea.

Jess removed his cramped fingers from her shoulders forcefully, and one by one. With a single motion of his hip and arm he shoved her out of the way and grabbed the wheel, easing the *Miss Santa Fe* around and out of the path of the larger vessel. Kelsey shouted into the microphone again, "Attention *Sea Wizard!* You are in violation of federal fishing regulations! Pull in your net! Pull in your net *now!*"

Jess settled the engines into idle, and he could hear the shouting from the opposite deck. There were at least four men and each of them expressed his outrage in his own inimitably colorful fashion, but the essence of it was, "Who the hell do you think you are?" and "What the hell do you think you're doing?"

Kelsey flung the microphone down and stalked out of the wheelhouse, her eyes blazing like fast-burning coals, and this time Jess knew the look. He swore sharply under his breath and dropped the anchor.

"I wouldn't if I were you," Craig murmured as Jess rushed past, and a moment later Jess wished he had listened to him.

There weren't four men, there were six, and each one of them looked as though he could have had a career as a prize-fighter. The two boats were so close that, except for the difference in height, one might have stepped from one deck to the other. And as Jess came out of the wheelhouse he was afraid that was exactly what was going to happen.

"No, you listen to *me!*" Kelsey was shouting, and her voice, buoyed by fury, cut sharply across the melee created by the men on the opposite deck even without the microphone. "*You're* the ones in trouble here! And you've got exactly thirty seconds to—"

The fury that erupted from the other deck drowned out not only her words, but the individual voices themselves. Jess, who had spent enough time with fishermen to know that a sense of humor was not among their strong points, particularly where their livelihood was concerned, muttered incredulously, "She's going to get us all killed."

"At least," agreed Dean. He had appeared at Jess's shoulder, in wet suit and dive gear. Jess barely spared him a glance, but moved cautiously toward Kelsey.

His eyes were on the other boat, measuring the odds if it came to a physical confrontation—and they did not, he had to admit, look good. One of the fishermen, a hard-muscled, dark-toothed man, had already swung one leg over the rail and was waving his fist, looking like an old-fashioned pirate preparing to board. It occurred to Jess that if he could shut Kelsey up they might all get out of here alive, but he realized almost immediately it would be easier to fight the pirates.

Preoccupied, as he was, with plans for self-defense, he never saw it coming. A sound split the air that registered a second later as a gunshot. He lunged toward Kelsey before he realized it was she who had fired; he grabbed her arm before he noticed that the pistol she held—a .22 caliber, just as she had said—was pointed straight up in the air. And when he realized that everyone—particularly the fishermen on the other boat—was very still, and very quiet, he slowly released her arm, and took a step back. When he saw the man with his leg over the rail cautiously ease back onto his own deck, it was all Jess could do to keep from grinning.

Kelsey said, "Now that I've got your attention, gentlemen, I just want to remind you of the laws regulating net size—laws that, unfortunately, you chose to ignore." As she spoke she lowered the pistol, but held it casually in her hand, propping her wrist on the rail. "Now I'm going to send a diver down to make sure you haven't trapped anything besides mackerel in that net, and if you have you're not only going to spend a lot of days onshore mending your net, you're going to be paying a hefty fine for every mammal that's damaged—and that's in addition to the fine you're already being levied for violating the regulations."

The captain of the vessel, still keeping a cautious eye on the pistol Kelsey held, returned, "I never heard of no rules like that! Who the hell are you, anyway?"

Kelsey's voice was calm and reasonable, but the passion that burned in her eyes and colored her face would have made even the most confident man think twice. "You are approaching a protected zone. You are fishing for mackerel in an area where dolphins feed on mackerel, and you're using standard-sized netting, which has been proven hazardous to the dolphin population. I don't know how to make it any clearer to you."

"Lady, I don't know what the hell you're talking about! I've been fishing these waters for fifteen years—"

"That's exactly the problem," Kelsey said tightly, and just then Dean broke the surface of the water. He pushed back his face mask and waved his arm.

"All clear!"

Kelsey turned her attention back to the fishing boat. "Well, gentlemen, it looks like you're in luck. But if I were you, I'd pull in that net and head for shore. You've already been reported on this violation, another one could mean your license. And if it happens to be me who catches you, you'll lose more than your license, I promise you."

Jess waited an interminable moment while the two stared each other down, and then the captain of the fishing vessel turned away. Kelsey remained at her post glaring across the deck at the fishing boat, and Jess went to help Dean on board.

Jess said casually, "I thought the net regulations only applied to tuna boats. And this area isn't protected against fishermen."

Kelsey did not reply, or even turn around, and it was Dean who answered, "Kelsey has this way of quoting regulations the way they *should* be, not necessarily the way they are." He unstrapped the scuba harness and pushed back his helmet. "Some people think it's cute."

Jess replied, just as pleasantly, "Yeah, I can see how they would." He helped Dean off with the air tank, then walked over to Kelsey.

"All right, Rambo, I'll take the sidearm." He leaned against the rail, hand extended, palm up. "I guess I should've made it clear automatic weapons are not considered standard gear. My mistake."

Her eyes flashed obstinacy and protest when she swung her gaze on him, but even her own righteous indignation could not blind her to the warning in Jess's face, or the cold fury simmering beneath his conversational tone. After a moment she reluctantly surrendered the weapon.

Jess checked to see that the safety was on, then tucked the pistol inside his waistband. "That was pretty fancy talking, Legs," he complimented her. "And damn fine steering."

She said cautiously, "Thanks."

He caught her gaze and held it. "But if you ever put my boat in that kind of danger again I'll personally see there's not enough left of you to use for bait, have you got that? This is not a goddamn Coast Guard cutter and I'm not getting hazardous duty pay and if you even *look* like you're thinking about pulling another stunt like that again I'm turning around and heading for shore. Do we understand each other?"

The color surged to her cheeks again. "Now, wait just a minute—"

"Do we understand each other?"

For an endless moment the two wills were locked in mortal combat. Jess could see what it cost her to finally be the one to move her gaze away, and to mutter, stiffly, "Yes."

Jess forced his shoulders to relax, and his voice. "Good," he said. "Because I want you to know that little episode took about ten years off my life. What do you say we get out of here while the rest of it is still worth living?''

For a moment she looked wary, and then Jess saw her release the tension with the same kind of forceful deliberation he had. She almost, but not quite, smiled. ''Right,'' she said.

Dean gave Jess a very odd look as he passed, but Jess barely noticed. For the next fifteen minutes he concentrated on nothing except breathing deeply, getting his boat out of harm's way and trying, very hard, not to think about how much he wanted to strangle Kelsey Morgan.

It took Kelsey about three hours to realize she'd been ''handled.'' No one, man or woman, had ever been able to do that before and when she realized how smoothly Jess Seward had managed it she almost laughed out loud with astonishment and admiration. She was used to getting what she wanted and doing so through nothing more than bull-like determination; she couldn't remember the last time she had surrendered anything as important as a weapon—or a principle—to anyone. Yet Jess had disarmed her in more ways than one, expertly and without bloodshed. And he had done it without even making her angry.

Of course he was furious with her, and she didn't blame him. He couldn't be expected to understand the kinds of things she had to deal with, or what was at stake, or the lengths to which she was sometimes forced to go in order to make a point. The fact of the matter was, no one could understand and Kelsey had never cared whether anyone did or not—just as she had never cared what anyone else thought about her actions or who was furious with her or why. But she didn't want Jess to be angry.

They anchored near the shallows, and she assigned Dean and Craig as the first dive team. She ached with jealousy to be in the water herself, but there were disadvantages to being team leader, and the first was that sense of noblesse oblige that required her to stay on board charting coordinates while her colleagues had all the fun.

She was too restless and nervous to sit at the workstation, listening to meaningless static hums from the radio receiver and speculating about the equally meaningless blips, bubbles and whines the hydrophone—a specialized underwater microphone—picked up. She kept thinking about the odds against Simba, about the odds against her finding Simba again exactly where she was supposed to be and about the consequences if she did not. She kept thinking about how anxiety had a way of disappearing in the thick, silent underwater world of slow-motion beauty, and she wondered impatiently where Dean and Craig were. They were allowed twenty minutes; they had been gone four. It seemed like four hours.

Jess was on deck, sipping a beer, looking out over the rail. After a moment Kelsey got up and left the wheelhouse.

She stood beside him, her back to the rail, leaning her weight casually on her elbows. "Listen," she said, "if you're still mad..."

"Mad?" He lifted the beer can to his lips and did not bother to turn to look at her. His tone was quiet and smooth, belying his words. "Damn right I'm still mad. I'm mad and amazed and glad as hell I don't ever have to see you again once we hit shore. If you can cause this much trouble on the open sea, I don't want to think what you could do in a riverfront alley. A man'd have to be a martial arts specialist just to take you to dinner."

"I was doing my job," she said impatiently. "If you'd just—"

"Your job is to impersonate a federal official and threaten innocent fishermen at gunpoint? Now you see if I'd've known that I *sure* wouldn't have taken this charter."

"Oh, don't give me that macho bull, okay? I hate it when men do that. Just because a woman can be tough doesn't mean your masculinity is threatened."

"Forget my masculinity, it was my *life* that was threatened back there." And then he did turn his head to look at her. "And what if those guys report us?" he demanded. "I'm the one who goes to jail, not you."

"You won't go to jail," she replied with a shrug. "And they won't report us. They're too scared *we're* going to report them."

She heard Jess draw a deep breath, and then, incredibly, he released it in a soft laugh. He gave a single shake of his head and drank from the can again. "Lady," he said, "you are something else."

Kelsey didn't want to say so, but so was he, and his laughter caused a thrill of pleasure to go through her, even if his words were not meant as a compliment. Another man might have tried to stop her that afternoon; he might have argued with her or tried to overpower her and turned a volatile situation into a deadly one with a display of masculine superiority. Jess had done exactly the right thing, though every male instinct he possessed must have warred against it. He had been there for her, ready to back her up if she needed it, but not interfering in what he didn't understand. And, as Kelsey looked back on the episode, she was amazed to realize that she must have known all along that she could count on him.

Kelsey couldn't remember ever having counted on anyone but herself before. Yet with Jess, she hadn't thought twice.

That line of thought was disturbing, and she veered away from it quickly. She said, "Have you ever done any diving around here?"

He gave her a dry, sidelong glance that acknowledged her change of subject, and took another sip of beer before answering, "You could say that. That's how I made my first million."

She returned a skeptical look and he added, "Of course, I didn't make it all for myself. But my share was enough to turn me into the independent businessman you see before you today."

She pushed away from the rail, half turning to stare at him. "You're serious."

He finished off the beer. "I was on the salvage team of the *Croydon* eight years ago . . . you might remember, that was before you bleeding hearts closed the site down to treasure hunters.''

Kelsey did remember. The *Croydon,* a nineteenth-century sunken freighter, had yielded one of the largest individual finds of the decade, and had, in fact, sparked all of the subsequent interest in treasure hunting around the Falpors, which had resulted in the area being restricted.

''We didn't close it down,'' she replied absently, still staring at him. ''We just made it harder to invade. How much did you get, anyway?''

He laughed, crumpling the beer can between his fingers before tossing it into the trash bin. ''Not nearly enough, take my word for it. Why?'' The spark in his eyes was like a random flash of sunshine on a murky deep sea as he turned to her. ''Planning to marry me for my money?''

But Kelsey just shook her head in slow amazement, frowning a little. ''You're never what I expect,'' she murmured.

And that spark in his eyes held her, caressed her, tingling like a jolt of electricity in the pit of her stomach as he replied, ''I guess that makes us even. Because believe me, neither are you.''

There was no foreseeing the moment that began to congeal between them, and no explaining it, either. He simply looked at her, and Kelsey became acutely aware of how close they were, and how the material of his shorts pulled tight across his buttocks when he lifted one foot to the rail, and how thick his hair was, styled by sun and wind and natural wave. She had made love to this man, but she had never touched his hair. She had never traced the shape of his jaw, following the smooth, sharp angle from ear to chin, or tasted the hot flesh in the hollow of his throat or held his face between her hands. She ached for the things she had not done, and then suddenly, sharply for the things she had, and the memory made her throat dry.

The worst part was that he was thinking, or feeling, the same thing. Had she been alone, the sensations would have been easier to ignore. But she wasn't. She could see it in his eyes.

And then he turned away, leaning on the rail again, looking out at the still, flat sea. She made herself follow his gaze for a moment, but inevitably her eyes were drawn back to his profile, to the faint shadow of reddish-blond beard on his cheek, to the shape of his shoulders, to the lean, skilled fingers now resting negligently on the rail, to the shape of his torso and the spareness of his waist, and below.

There should be laws, she decided, about just how well a man's clothing could shape his body. Except that it had nothing to do with his clothes, and she suddenly couldn't remember why it had been so important that they resume a professional relationship for the remainder of the trip.

But she knew she had better remember, and fast.

She said, a little thickly, "What I came out to tell you was—well, thanks, I guess. For acting like you had some sense this afternoon."

"It seemed to me one of us should." And though she could see he didn't want to, he moved his eyes back to her. "Act like he had some sense, that is."

"Right," she said. But neither one of them seemed to be acting as though he had any sense at all at that moment. Jess's gaze was so intense it seemed to give off heat, and a fine dew of perspiration formed between her breasts and around her waistband.

He said, "You did a hell of a job handling the boat." He lowered his foot from the rail and turned to fully face her. He didn't touch her, but they were so close the hem of her overshirt brushed the hem of his shorts, and involuntarily she tightened her stomach muscles, which were only a fraction of an inch away from contact with his. But she didn't step back, nor did she have any desire to.

She said, "I told you I could."

"You didn't lie." His gaze moved down, touching her breasts, and her nipples hardened. "You didn't lie about the gun, either." He brought his eyes back to hers. "I really hate that in a woman."

"What?" The air was stifling, and her voice was breathless.

"If a woman can do something as well as—or better than—a man, she ought to have the decency to keep quiet about it."

"I really hate that in a man."

"It figures you would."

The atmosphere was so thick between them now it practically throbbed. And then his fingers touched hers, sliding against her palm, winding between her fingers, tightening. And he said, "I'll tell you something else." There was an odd husky tone to his voice, and his eyes were smoky dark, sea lit. "You scared the hell out of me this afternoon. Not because I was worried about myself, or the boat—which I was—but because I was worried about you. I'm not used to worrying about anybody else and I don't much like the feeling so don't do it again, okay?"

An odd sensation trembled through Kelsey, and it was more than the strong pull of sexual desire, or the heat generated by the grip of his fingers around hers. Had anyone ever worried about her before? Why should it make her feel so weak, so confused and breathless to think that he had?

She searched his eyes a little hesitantly. "I can take care of myself."

The small muscles around his eyes relaxed, almost forming a smile. "You think I don't know that? That only means I not only get to worry, I get to feel like a fool for worrying. The good news is, of course, that if I ever get into trouble I know who to call."

She started to laugh, softly, and it was more of a feeling than a sound; it rippled through her in an unfurling wave of simple pleasure, glowing in her skin and tingling in her fingertips. She found Jess's other hand and wound her fingers around it. "This is crazy," she said. "I really do like you."

He smiled, leaning forward until their abdomens touched, and then their chests. The pleasure of his nearness and of her laughter dissolved into something more intense, an almost painful awareness, a breathtaking, aching expectation and need. His smile faded, and so did hers as they looked at each other. Their fingers tightened.

He said, "How long do the divers have?"

"Twenty minutes." Her voice was a little hoarse.

He moved close and she thought he was going to kiss her; every sense leaped in anticipation of it. But instead he merely rested his forehead lightly, briefly against hers. His eyes closed. "You're right about one thing," he said. "This is crazy."

He moved away, releasing her hands. "We had a deal," he reminded her. His expression was masked, but the muscles in his face were strained; his eyes questioning.

Kelsey swallowed hard. "If the divers weren't due back . . . would we still have a deal?"

He looked at her for a moment, then moved his gaze back to the sea. He didn't answer. And later, after she had a chance to think about it, Kelsey was glad neither of them had put it into words.

Seven

Two more days passed with no sign of the dolphin, Simba, and they were among the most harrowing, nerve-racking days of Jess's life. It came as no surprise to Jess to learn that when Kelsey was anxious or upset she made certain she did not suffer alone; her snappish mood cowed her two colleagues and it amused Jess to see how far they would go to stay out of her way. But it wasn't Kelsey's temper that wore on his nerves. It was Kelsey herself.

As much as the other two men exerted themselves to avoid her, Jess went out of his way to stay near her— to watch her, to cross her, even to irritate her, just for the pleasure it gave him to match wits with her, to see her eyes blaze, and then, occasionally, if he pushed hard enough and did it just right, to make her laugh. He had never known it could be such a challenge to interact with a woman on a nonphysical level; to test her, to try to predict her, to simply think about her. And when he realized how much time he was spending thinking about her, the strain on his nerves really began.

He thought about Kelsey with exasperation and impatience and admiration and amazement; he thought about her with a hunger that hadn't really gone away since the first night. He thought about her with anger and frustration because she *wouldn't* go away, and he wondered if any other woman would ever hold any appeal for him again.

He had taken to stringing a hammock up on deck at night, and after the others had retired he lay there, watching the darkened porthole of the forward cabin and playing the familiar game: he wondered what she wore to bed at night, he wondered if she was thinking about him, he wondered what would happen if he got up, and walked through the wheelhouse, and pushed open the cabin door... And that was the worst part. Because he knew what would happen. And the effort it took not to get up was so great that the strain actually left his muscles aching in the morning.

The last thing he needed was a woman like Kelsey Morgan complicating his life. But without even trying she had already complicated it more than he would have thought it was possible for any one female to do.

In the early hours of the morning of the fifth day at sea, Jess felt the engines start up. His feet were on the deck before his eyes were fully open, he grabbed his shirt and pulled it over his head as he ran, and when he burst into the wheelhouse Kelsey was at the controls.

"Don't give me any trouble," she said irritably, without even glancing back at him.

"Like it would do any good?" He pushed his fingers through his hair and leaned one shoulder against the bulkhead as his pounding heart slowly settled down.

It was barely dawn; the morning star hung like a jewel in a dark gray sky and the glow on the horizon was so faint it could have been wishful thinking. He glanced at the papers and charts spread out all over the work shelf, the litter of soda cans and candy wrappers on the floor, and he inquired, "How long have you been up planning this mutiny, anyway?"

"I don't think I went to bed."

He felt a tug in his chest that was half sympathy, half wonder. Her hair was loosely pinned up in an unruly mass of curls, and he could see the tension in the slim line of her neck. Her shoulders were slumped with fatigue beneath the long-sleeved cotton knit shirt she wore, her feet were bare and her shorts wrinkled. His instinct was to go over to her and begin massaging her neck and shoulders. Instead he tested all the soda cans until he found one with some liquid left in it, and he took a drink. He said, "Want to tell me where we're going?"

"I don't know." Her voice was short, but it was with fatigue and worry, not anger. "I picked up something on the receiver that could have been Simba's radio tag . . . it sounded like her frequency. But it wasn't very clear. Maybe I didn't hear anything at all.''

The uncertainty in her voice bothered him, making her seem too vulnerable, too tired . . . almost defeated. He wanted to take her in his arms, to tell her not to worry, that it didn't matter . . . he wanted to lead her to bed and lie down with her and hold her, and make love to her while the sun rose. But he wouldn't do that. Mostly because, to Kelsey, it did matter.

He nudged her shoulder firmly with the back of his hand. ''I'll take over. You get on the receiver, let me know if you pick up anything.''

Kelsey hesitated, then glanced up at him. Her eyes were so tired they burned, and she really couldn't remember how long she'd been awake, poring over maps, charts and notes, scanning the frequencies . . . But looking at him was like a dose of caffeine, a rush of adrenaline, and she forgot to be tired.

He was wearing a hooded sweatshirt and frayed denim cutoffs that were soft and rumpled; the same shorts he had worn that other night, and beneath them, only flesh. His hair was tousled and his jaw stubbled and his eyes drowsy. He brought the intimacy of nighttime into the well-lit wheelhouse, the innocence of sleep and the scent of sexuality and the combination was faintly arousing, definitely distracting. And distractions were the one thing she could not afford.

She glanced back at the controls, hesitating another moment, then stood up. ''Yeah, okay. Somebody ought to watch the sonar, too. Just stay on this course, we're going to veer around the other side of the island. And be careful, there's a reef—''

He gave her a dry look as he slid into the chair she vacated. "I know where the reefs are."

Kelsey went to the workstation and sat down, holding the radio headphones to one ear and dividing her visual attention between the sonar screen and the view from the forward window. Not that she expected to see much in the near dark, but watching was a habit. And gazing toward the forward window also gave her an excellent view of Jess's strong back and shoulders, muscles flexing and relaxing beneath the soft material of the navy sweatshirt.

After a time Jess said, "If you don't find this dolphin you're looking for, it's not the end of the world, you know."

She frowned as she turned her attention back to the sonar. "Yeah? For whom?"

"We must have spotted half a dozen dolphins since we've been here. The other guys seem to be finding plenty to do—even without the sleeping sharks. So what's so special about this one dolphin?"

"She's mine," Kelsey replied briefly.

Jess turned to look at her, one eyebrow lifted in a way that made Kelsey very uncomfortable. "I thought you didn't have personal relationships with marine life."

Again she frowned. "I don't. What I mean is, she was my first project when I came to the institute—the reason I came, really. Graphton got her from a marine park that was closing down, and I designed the program to resocialize her to the wild, and then release her. If we were successful—which we were—and if she survived, the final phase of the study was to observe her in her natural environment.''

Something about the way she said the words ''if she survived,'' the way her face tightened and her eyes shifted away, told Jess everything he ever needed to know about why this expedition was so important to her. He said, ''How long did you work with her?''

''A year and a half.''

''It must have been hard, letting her go.''

She looked for a moment as though she wanted to deny ever having fallen victim to such sentimental weakness, but he had already seen the truth in her eyes, and she knew it.

''Yeah,'' she admitted, ''It was. She taught us so much more than we could ever teach her, and all the time I was wondering if I was doing the right thing, wondering if I was sending her to her death... wondering if she'd be happy.'' She glanced at him defensively, half expecting him to laugh and a little surprised to find nothing but interest in his eyes. ''I know it sounds stupid, but dolphins are very family-oriented mammals, and Simba would be an orphan out there. We didn't know how others of her own species would treat her, and this is our only chance to find out. It's our only chance to find out a lot of things.''

And then, because she was sure that sounded entirely too sentimental, she added, ''Of course, if I can complete this project I can pretty much write my own ticket from here on out." Her attention quickened as she thought she picked up an echo on the receiver. "Twenty degrees starboard, okay?"

He made the course change without comment. Then, "What would that ticket be?"

She listened, but the echo seemed to have faded. She looked back at him. "Honestly?"

He eased back on the thruster, letting the engines settle into an easy pace, then swiveled his chair around so that he could keep one eye on her and the other on the wheel. His expression was an invitation to the kind of candor that Kelsey rarely shared with other people, but something about the quiet dawn, the hum of the engines, and Jess, simply being who he was, made confidence easy.

She said, "My own lab. You know, like Cousteau's *Calypso,* a floating marine lab. To be able to just set sail for anywhere, anytime I wanted to, and stay as long as I needed to. To study what needs to be studied and give it as much time as it deserves without having to worry about some suit pulling me in early... And to wake up every morning and know there's a new piece of ocean waiting for me to explore, and that this might be the day and I might be the person who discovers something no one else has ever found before..." She was starting to wax rhapsodic, as she often did when she talked about her private dreams, and she stopped herself, embarrassed.

But Jess was smiling—not at her; with her. He said,
"Sounds like the life to me. I don't guess you'll be
needing a captain on this boat of yours?"

She smiled. "It'll already have one. Me."

"And all this from one dolphin?"

She shrugged. "Well, maybe not all. But once I
publish my findings I'll be receiving a hell of a lot of
attention, and that's just another way of saying documentary films, private sponsorship..." And she
smiled, unable to keep the glow of a secret hope from
her eyes now. "Let's just say it's a start. A *big* start."

Then she looked at him, and added in a far more
neutral tone, "So now you see why I didn't want those
fishermen dragging their nets around here. They
could've bagged a million-dollar dolphin."

"Yeah, I see."

But the way he said it, and the way he smiled made
Kelsey think he saw more than she wanted him to, and
she looked away uncomfortably.

The ocean was vast and empty, and the receiver was
silent. Kelsey tried, once again, not to think about the
odds. She tried not to think about the fishermen. And
she tried not to worry.

She watched the sonar and the map of the ocean
floor, but it was instinct more than anything else that
told her when they had reached the area of the Falpors characterized by submerged caves and erratic
floor drop-offs. And it was that same instinct that told
her this was the direction from which that first uncertain radio signal had come and this was the place it was
most likely to appear again.

She looked up to tell Jess to cut the engines and allow the boat to drift, but before she could form a single word he had done just that. She stared at him, and he explained with a shrug of his shoulders, "Looks like a likely spot. If you want to go on we can, but after a few years with the sea you get a feel for these things. I think if you're going to pick up anything on that receiver, here's the best place to do it."

She turned back to the workstation, swallowing back her amazement. "Yeah, right. We'll give it a shot."

Jess stood up, pressing both hands into his back as he stretched. Kelsey didn't mean to, but she couldn't help noticing the way the tendons in his legs lengthened, tightening in his thighs.

He said, "I'll listen for a while if you want to run down to the galley and make coffee."

A prickle of irritation crossed her face. "You run down to the galley and make coffee."

"Too far."

"Too bad."

"You got anything over there with caffeine in it?" He started rummaging around among the litter on the workstation, shaking cans and discarding candy wrappers.

"Hey!" She struck out at him, as he came very near to spilling a half-empty can of cola over the maps she had spread out. "Why don't you go back to bed?"

"Just like a woman." He moved aside some manuals on the top shelf and retrieved a package of pea-

nuts that Kelsey had not discovered during the night.
"They use you then they toss you away."

She nudged the cola can toward him. "Do you want
the rest of this or not?"

"It's flat. And warm." But he took it anyway, and
sat down on the corner of the work shelf, his knee
swinging near Kelsey's elbow. "How far is that receiver supposed to pick up, anyway?"

"Two miles, but you never know." She shifted the
earphone to the other ear. It would have been simpler
to put the headset on, but if she did that she wouldn't
be able to talk to Jess. And she didn't really want him
to leave. "The transmitter has never been tested this
long before, not under marine conditions."

Jess turned his gaze toward the window, which was
frosted with mist from their wake. "Big ocean," he
commented.

And she agreed bleakly, "Yes."

Kelsey had long since observed that the minutes that
separated nighttime from dawn were like no other on
the clock; night lingered in shades of navy blue and
deep gray while dawn struggled feebly to push its pale
green light over the horizon, and the minutes turned
into hours. Waves slapped softly against the hull and
a sea mist rose in the warming air, took shape, and
blew away. The boat rocked and shifted aimlessly, a
victim of the current. For Kelsey, who had spent her
share of endless dawns wrestling with some work-
related problem, this was the loneliest and most des-
olate time of times. She was suddenly intensely glad
not to have to spend this dawn alone.

Jess got up, walked to the console, hesitated, then returned to the workstation. He glanced at the sonar, and at the maps. He got up again.

"What?" Kelsey demanded, watching him. "What are you so nervous about?"

"Nothing. I was just thinking about dropping the anchor. It can be dangerous, drifting like this."

"Don't be ridiculous. The nearest land mass is thirty feet below us."

"Still, I don't like to drift."

She gave a snort of laughter. "That sounds funny, coming from a man who doesn't even have a permanent mailing address."

There was a twinkle in his eye as he glanced at her. "So. A philosopher, are you?" But he resumed his seat near her on the work shelf, and allowed the boat to continue to drift.

She shrugged. "Just observant. A man who's afraid of getting lost might be smart to stay put."

He chuckled, sipping the warm soda. "I like that. But there's a difference between being afraid and being cautious, you know."

"Not much."

"Speaks the woman who doesn't know the meaning of the word fear—or caution."

"Sure I do. I'm 'cautious' about a lot of things."

She put the earphones down for a minute, rubbing the back of her neck. Instinctively Jess lifted his hand to perform the service for her, then let it drop. But it was an effort to keep his tone casual, and his eyes off the slim, arched line of her neck.

"What are you afraid of?" he asked.

Kelsey started to pick up the earphone again, but then changed her mind. She didn't think she could stand listening to the emptiness anymore. "Failing," she said quietly. She turned away from the earphone and looked out over the sea, propping her chin on her folded hands. "That's what I'm afraid of right now."

"That's not fear—nobody wants to lose. Tell me something I don't know."

His voice was smooth and easy, with just a trace of a Midwestern accent that was comfortable on the ear. Of all the things Kelsey had admired about him, she had never noticed how mesmeric his voice was before. Or perhaps it was simply the quality of the dawn, the quiet and the intimacy, that made confidence easy.

She was silent for a moment, looking out over the gray-green ocean. And then she said, "I drowned when I was four years old. Playing in a reservoir, I'd been out ten minutes before they found me. I was terrified of the water after that. But as soon as I got out of the hospital, my dad started me in swim lessons at the Y. It was a nightmare. I hated it all the way through the advanced class . . . and then one day I discovered I wasn't scared anymore.

"When I joined my first scuba group I was just a teenager, but I still should've known better. I talked some guys into going with me to explore some caves a few miles out from where we usually dived. Naturally I got separated from them, lost in an underwater cave. My guide rope got fouled and while I was trying to free it I stirred up so much silt I couldn't tell top from bottom...I don't guess I've ever been so scared. By the time they found me my air was almost gone and I never wanted to see another cave...the next week I started working toward certification in cave diving. It's still not my favorite thing to do, but I can handle it.''

She hesitated, uncertain whether she wanted to go on. "I guess...the one thing I'm really afraid of is the dark." And she made a quick, dismissing gesture that indicated their present surroundings. "Not dark, but *dark*. The bottom-of-the-sea dark, the ice-cold dark, the all-alone dark where you can't see a foot in front of you even with your dive light and you never know what's hiding in the shadows and your partner might be right behind you but you're still all alone." She took a breath. "That's what I'm afraid of. The dark."

She could feel him, very close to her; closer then he had been before though physically he had not moved. She could feel his gaze, thoughtful and gentle, drawing her in, causing her, inevitably, to turn and meet his eyes. Sea-softened eyes, as sober as the day that dawned so reluctantly around them. Beneath those eyes she felt stripped and vulnerable.

She said, forcing a tight smile, "Now your turn. What are you afraid of?"

He almost, but not quite, returned her smile. His gaze was like a caress, making her skin tingle. "Besides sharks?"

She nodded.

He dropped his eyes to the soda can in his hand, and then put it aside. He looked at her, and said, "You."

Her heart began to pound, slowly and steadily. A pinkish glow suffused the sky, but that could not have accounted for the heat that seemed to creep into the room, charging the very air with a pulsing anticipation.

She said unsteadily, "Me? Why?"

He lifted his hand, lightly brushing the mass of curls atop her head, drifting down to encircle her neck. His touch was like velvet and steel, firm, gentle. The warmth of his touch penetrated the top of her spinal column and radiated downward throughout her midsection. And his eyes were like sunshine through fog.

He said quietly, "I think...because you're the only real woman I've ever known."

She wanted to, but she couldn't look away from him. The pressure on the back of her neck increased, ever so slightly, and his other hand slipped beneath her arm, urging her to stand. She didn't resist as he got to his feet and drew her with him, pulling her close. His bare thighs were against hers, her breasts drawing in the heat of his chest. She rested her hands on his arms, sinewy muscle beneath cottony-soft material. She moved her hands upward over his biceps, around his shoulders. She lifted her face and tasted the kiss of his breath on her face, and then his lips, closing on hers, drawing on hers with a tenderness that made her tremble. She sank into him, aching for him, and when she parted her lips she tasted him inside her, slowly, thoroughly, tasting and exploring and needing; time stood still.

When they parted it was with reluctance and uncertainty. The passion that was no stranger to them took on a new and subtler form, as thoroughly permeating and just as powerful as anything they had known before—yet more. Kelsey felt weak against him, aching not just for what his body could give her but for his warmth, his voice, his smile, his touch, his simple nearness. She could feel his heart beat against her breast, and see the pulse in his throat. She touched that pulse, a strong male throb of heat and power against her fingertips. She lifted her gaze to his and saw the same unmasked hunger, the same subtle confusion that was in her own.

Her chest hurt with the unsteadiness of her breathing, and she could feel his own rhythmic breaths against her cheek. She wanted to pull away but she couldn't. She wanted to kiss him again, to sink into his arms and let herself be lost there, but she wouldn't. Danger hummed a thin high warning bell in the back of her mind.

Except it wasn't in her mind. She felt his hands tighten on her waist a moment before she recognized the significance of what she was hearing. Still, unwilling to step away from him, she only half turned toward the workstation, her hands drifting down to rest against his chest. Then he said, "Kelsey..."

And she released a breath. She wasn't imagining it. She snatched up the earphone but her heart was suddenly pounding so hard she could barely hear. She put the headset on and held her breath, concentrating. She felt Jess's hand on her shoulder and she lifted her hand, gripping his fingers.

There was no mistake. The signal came through loud and clear.

"My God," she breathed. "It's her. It is."

For another moment she listened, her eyes widening with delight and disbelief, and then she broke into a laugh of sheer, incredulous joy. "Listen!" she cried. She snatched off the headset and held it out to him. "It's so clear you can practically see it! She must be right under the boat!"

And then abruptly she jumped up, running out of the wheelhouse and onto the deck. Jess was right behind her as she swung one foot over the rail and onto the ladder.

"What are you doing?" he demanded. But there was laughter in his voice and amazement in his face.

She balanced on the ladder outside the boat, holding on to the rail with one hand, and Jess caught her waist through the rail, steadying her as she knelt down. She slapped her hand against the water, splashing cold spray on her face and dampening her shirt. She barely noticed.

"Do you think she'll remember you?" Jess inquired incredulously. "After all this time?"

"Of course not. She's just a dolphin." But she slapped the water again.

She saw the shadow beneath the water and a cry of wonder surged to her throat. An instant later a sleek gray snout broke the surface of the water, thrusting upward to meet Kelsey on her level. Jess's hand tightened on her waist and his hoarse exclamation of delight echoed her own.

"Simba!" Kelsey cried. "It's her, it is!" She stretched out her hands to stroke the velvety head. "She's here, she's okay—and she remembers me!"

She gasped with laughter as Simba dropped beneath the water with a playful splash of her tail that soaked not only Kelsey, but Jess as well. He was laughing as he pulled her back over the rail, and she turned into his embrace, crying, "Do you believe that? Do you know the odds? I found her—after all this time, I found her!"

His eyes were twinkling as he looked down at her, dancing with amazement and affection and pride. "Why so surprised? That's what you set out to do."

From behind them Dean called, "What's all the excitement?"

And Craig, "Is anything wrong?"

"Simba!" Kelsey cried. She pushed away from Jess and gripped the rail, excitedly searching the starburst dawn. Scarlet and yellow sunlight streaked the sky and rippled through the ocean, a dramatic backdrop for what happened in the next instant. "Look!"

Twenty feet away from the boat Simba broke the surface of the water and leaped high in the air, performing an acrobatic dance of joy that was only a reflection of what Kelsey felt. Distantly she heard Dean's and Craig's exclamations and congratulations, but they were drowned out by her own whoop of laughter as she turned to Jess. He caught her up in his arms and she threw back her head and laughed, because in his arms was the only place she wanted to be, and because laughter was the only way to express even a small portion of the happiness she felt.

Eight

There weren't enough hours in that day. Kelsey lay on
her bunk that night with her mind busily playing back
pictures—diving with Simba, playing with Simba, ex-
amining Simba, filming Simba; the notes she'd made,
the things she'd learned, the things she had yet to learn
and mustn't forget to write down... Yet, as exciting
as finding Simba was, only half her mind was occu-
pied with the dolphin. The other half was preoccupied, most disturbingly, with Jess.

She couldn't remember ever telling another man the
things she had told Jess that morning. She could not
recall feeling with another man what she had felt when
Jess took her in his arms—the comfort, the vulnera-
bility, the need that went beyond sex. The sense of

being safe, and the hunger for something she couldn't even define... It was all crazy, and too much for her overworked brain to sort out tonight. She wished she had somebody to talk to. And the craziest part was that the person she wanted to talk to was Jess.

. It was warm inside the cabin, and she was restless, keyed up. She had slept so little the night before she didn't dare get up and spend another night working. But tossing and turning on the hot, rumpled sheets was not doing her any good, either. She sat up on her knees and pushed open the porthole over the bed, expecting a cool breeze to soothe her into sleep. But the air outside was as warm and still as it was inside.

"Storm's brewing." Jess's voice spoke out of the shadows.

Kelsey's heartbeat quickened as she turned her head. She knew he often slept on deck, and more than once she had envied him his hammock in the open breeze. Tonight was one of those nights.

She said, "I guess two solid weeks of good weather was too much to expect." She still couldn't see him; the night was cloudy and the deck was dark. "It won't be much of a storm, though. The sea's too calm."

He said, "A little rain will cool the air. Don't you ever sleep?"

"It's too hot." She searched the shadows, straining her eyes. "Where are you?"

"About four feet to your left."

She still couldn't see him. "What are you doing?"

There was amusement in his voice. "Lying down. Do you want to know what I'm wearing?"

A low chuckle played in her throat as she made out the faintest shape of the hammock, stretched between the rail and the bulkhead. "No thanks, I'd rather let my imagination run wild."

And then, on a mischievous impulse, she added, "You can tell me something, though. Do you have a tattoo on your shoulder?"

"No." His voice brimmed with amusement. "What about you?"

"No." She was irrationally disappointed. "No tattoos, anywhere?"

"Not a single one. I'm a coward when it comes to needles. Sorry."

She stifled a sigh. "That's okay. I just figured you for the tattoo type. I told you, I have terrible judgment when it comes to people."

After a moment he said, "So. Was everything the way you expected with the dolphin?"

"The fact that she survived this long was more than I expected," Kelsey confessed. "But otherwise . . . it's really amazing. Did you notice how anxious she was to show off all her tricks? The fact that she even remembers them is incredible enough, but she almost acted as though she had been just waiting all this time for someone to come along and give her the right cues—like she was happy to be performing again! For an animal that's been so completely socialized to humans to survive as well as she's done in the wild is not a usual thing. Of course, I was disappointed to see she was alone. I'd hoped she would be adopted into a family—and maybe she has been. One day's observation is hardly enough and she could be a part of any one of the schools around here. But one of the main things I wanted to do was compare her language now to what it was before, and to do that effectively I really need to see her interact with other dolphins...."

Suddenly she caught herself, realizing she was getting carried away and that she could go on like that for hours if he didn't stop her...and he wouldn't stop her. She gave a rueful little shake of her head, even though she knew he couldn't see, and she accused, "You're smiling, aren't you?"

"Just a little. I like to hear you talk about your fish."

"Mammals."

"Just the thing to make me sleepy."

"Don't get too comfortable. It's starting to rain."

He swore softly as the first light drops pattered on the deck. "One of the few disadvantages to not having a roof over your head," he said.

Kelsey heard the creak of ropes and the sound of his feet on deck as he got up and began to take down the hammock. She rested her chin on the porthole opening. "Need any help?"

"Yeah. You can come out here and take this down while I get out of the rain."

"This wouldn't even be a good fog in San Diego. You won't melt."

"Well, at least it's cooling off."

She heard more movements, the opening and closing of a storage locker. His footsteps were muffled now by the soft whisper of the rain, another dimension to the rise and fall of the ocean's sighs. And when a moment passed and she heard nothing more, Kelsey said uncertainly, "Jess?"

"Yeah, Legs." His voice wasn't far away. "Get some shut-eye. I'm going below."

She wished she could see his face. Her hands tightened on the rim of the porthole and her heart picked up a sluggish, squeezing rhythm. She said softly, "There's room for two in here."

He didn't answer. She waited, straining for a response, almost holding her breath . . . but there was none. He hadn't heard. He had already gone. It was probably for the best.

After a moment she sank back into the room, feeling a little foolish, a little relieved, and very disappointed. She left the porthole open to the sound of the rain and the marginally cooler air, and leaned back against the headboard, drawing up her knees. She couldn't sleep now. It was foolish to even try.

When she looked up Jess was standing in the doorway, a silhouette against the faint glow of LED lights in the wheelhouse behind him. Kelsey straightened out her legs slowly. She said, as steadily as she could, "What took you so long?"

Jess stood there for a moment, letting his eyes adjust to the darkness, drinking her in. She looked like something from an expensive perfume ad, sitting in the middle of the rumpled bed with her hair wild around her shoulders, wearing a skinny gray tank top that barely skimmed her waist and cotton bikini panties of the same color. He found the two-inch expanse of skin between the bottom of her shirt and the top of her panties instantly riveting, sharply erotic. And he answered huskily, "What took you so long to ask?"

Kelsey drew in her breath and held it, deep in her chest, as he shut the door behind him, then came toward her. He wasn't wearing a shirt, and she could see the faint gleam of rain on his chest, moisture darkening his hair. A few feet before the bed he stopped, and she released her breath in a slow soft whisper as he unfastened his shorts, and let them drop. Then he wasn't wearing anything at all.

The bed creaked slightly with his weight as he knelt astride her thighs. His skin was cool and damp with rain; droplets of moisture clung to his hair. Her fingers were unsteady as they moved lightly over his arms and his chest, cupping his neck, drifting restlessly down his back. His eyes were like dark jewels, his face softened by shadows. She wanted to simply look at him, to touch him. She thrust her fingers into his hair, treasuring its thick, silky texture, discovering the heat at the back of his neck, the shape of his shoulders, the knobs of his spine.

He bent his head, and with the slightest of pressure on her shoulders, he pushed her back onto the bed. Her muscles were like wax, melting at his touch. For a moment he lingered over her, his face filling her vision, and she could feel him, strong in his arousal, against her thigh. Then he leaned back, and hooked his fingers beneath her panties, slipped them off.

She could hear his breathing, slow and measured, and she forced hers into the same rhythm. Her heart was shattering in her chest, her skin flaming, her muscles trembling. He stroked the inside of her thighs, feather touches from apex to knee, then he dipped his head and traced the path of his fingers with the stream of his breath, and she bit back a cry of pleasure as he repeated the caress with his tongue.

He thrust his hands beneath her shirt, pushing it upward, cupping her breasts. His skin wasn't cool anymore; it was hot, blazing like hers. She kissed him, tasting him greedily, smothering her cries of pleasure inside his mouth. He moved away for a moment, to drag her shirt over her head, then he covered her with his body, drinking of her, making her dizzy. Making her ache for him.

The blind urgency that had dictated their first encounter was still present, still as strong, still as combustible and wildly unpredictable. But this time they were prepared for it. This time they would not let the frenzy of need rob them of the exquisite pleasure they found in each other; this time they would not cheat themselves—or each other—of all they had to share.

Kelsey made love with the same kind of passion she did everything else, holding nothing back, throwing caution to the wind. That was the passion that kept Jess awake at night, that caused his blood to thrum just looking at her at odd moments during the day; the passion that blazed in her eyes when she ordered a fishing boat out of her waters at gunpoint, the passion that glowed in her face when she talked about the sea, the passion of joy that had radiated from every part of her when she first saw Simba ... That was the passion that was turned toward him now and he drank it in, he thrived on it, he let it strip his senses and take his judgment and set his soul on fire. Because what he wanted from her was deeper than sex and more powerful than desire; it was the very essence of life. And that was what he wanted to give to her.

When he entered her it was slowly, drawing out the sensation, watching her eyes, watching himself become a part of her, feeling himself drown within her. Her heartbeat, pounding against his. Her fingers tightening on his and her mouth opening beneath his... They blended together, pieces of a broken puzzle fitting together and becoming whole. And even more than the physical sensation was that certainty, that rightness, of being a part of her. She made him want to possess her, to claim her, to mark this woman, this wonder they created together, as his own for all time; only her, only him. He held her face in his hands and looked into her eyes, as he buried himself deep within her.

Kelsey clasped him to her, rising to meet his thrust, drawing him deeper inside her as she thought, *It was never like this. Never...* There was something magical about the two of them together, something explosive and all-fulfilling and *right*. Something she had not expected and had not wanted but nonetheless couldn't deny, and that was why their first encounter had shaken her so badly, that was why—though it seemed impossible now, impossible and stupid and unnecessarily brutal—she had made herself stay away from him.

Because that very rightness frightened her, and because as the waves of need intensified into waves of blinding, helpless, rushing pleasure, because as she muffled her cries against his shoulder and kissed his face and tasted his mouth and inhaled his breath and because as she lay, trembling in his arms with his lips brushing kisses on her hair all she could think was, with a kind of fierce desperation, *I love you. I love you...* And it took more discipline than she thought she possessed not to say it out loud.

A long time later their breathing steadied, heartbeats slowed. The perspiration that slickened their bodies began to cool, and Jess pulled a sheet over them. The madness receded, but did not disappear.

They lay together, cocooned, fingers entwined, listening to the purr of rain on the deck. The boat swayed gently, imitating the rhythm their bodies had taken a short while ago. Jess kissed her fingers. "Ah, honey," he said softly. "This is crazy."

She whispered, "I know."

He looked down at her, brushing her hair back from her eyes with their entwined fingers. "Not this," he corrected. "Waiting so long. Especially when we knew..."

"Yes." Speaking was as easy as breathing, when she echoed his thoughts. "We knew."

Because what they knew was not only the time they had wasted, the pleasure they had lost, but the danger that confronted them now. Nothing as perfect as what they shared came without a price, and the payment would be demanded in another week, when they

docked again in Charleston, and had to say goodbye.
Kelsey had never dreaded losing a lover before. And
neither had Jess.

Kelsey looked at him, loving the shape of his jaw,
the soft brightness of his eyes, the thick curl of light
hair that rested on the pillow. She couldn't help smiling. Just looking at him made her happy... and sad.

She said, "I fantasized about you, you know."

His eyes narrowed with a smile. "Oh, yeah?"

She nodded. "One of those 'be careful what you
wish for' scenarios, I guess. But..." And she sighed,
snuggling deeper into the crook of his arm. "I never
thought it would be like this."

He chuckled softly. "I fantasized about you, too."

She glanced up at him. "What?"

"What you wore to bed, mostly."

"Disappointed?"

He dropped a slow kiss on her neck. "Only that I
don't even fantasize that good."

Kelsey shifted her position, looking up at the ceiling. "Of course," she said carefully, "it's just sex."

There was something odd about his voice, a little
guarded, as he agreed, "Right."

"It'll wear off in a week or two."

"Sure."

She looked at him, and saw the lie in his eyes, even
as he saw it in hers. An ache started in her chest, and
she looked away. "This morning you told me I was the
only real woman you'd ever met. It's funny. You
started out as a daydream, that first day I saw you on

the dock. And you turned out to be the most real man I've ever known.''

His head turned on the pillow to look at her, his breath brushed her cheek. He said quietly, "I don't want to be your hero, Kelsey."

She turned her face on the pillow, a fraction of an inch from his. "Nobody wants a real-life hero," she said, a little hoarsely. "All that riding off into the sunset—it could start to get on your nerves."

"And neither one of us is the kind to ever pass up a sunset."

She whispered, "No."

He turned his head, looking up at the ceiling, and after a moment, so did she. The rain pattered. The waves lapped against the hull. The boards groaned softly. And after a long time Jess said, "This isn't going to be easy, is it?"

Kelsey didn't answer. She didn't have to.

Nine

There was nothing easy about the following days. Jess spent hours watching her, doing nothing but watching her, filling his head with her: Kelsey, squinting against the sun, giving orders to Dean and Craig, laughing with her dolphin when she thought no one was looking, brisk and humorless as she worked with the animal or recorded her notes. Kelsey in her wet suit, knifing beneath the water, Kelsey in her swimsuit with her wet hair clinging to her shoulders and sparkling in the sun, kneeling at the rail and slapping her hand on the water, Kelsey smelling of salt and sea... Pictures of her, sounds of her, enough to last a lifetime.

He looked at her and he marveled over how a woman so unfeminine could be so powerfully sensuous, and he realized he had only been defining feminine by the wrong terms all these years. He listened to her dictate her notes into a recorder and he wondered what he possibly thought he could have in common with a woman whose job it was to take life's simplest pleasures—dolphin play, reef diving, watching the colors of the sea—and turn them into complicated scientific theorems. Then he wondered how anyone could fail to be fascinated by the way she saw things, and the way she explained them, and the way she made *him* see everything in a new light. Just being near her exhausted him and exhilarated him and challenged him and enlightened him and he wondered how much longer he could possibly stand it before demanding his old, easy, uncomplicated life back—the life he was in charge of, the life into which no one else could intrude. And then he wondered how long it would take him to get over her, and if he ever would.

Every night he told himself he would not go to her bed, and every night he forgot that promise as soon as it was made. And every time they made love she became more inextricably entwined inside him; he lost another part of himself to her.

Two days were left of the voyage, and the sensation of time running out hung like a lead weight over their heads.

Jess didn't like it when she dived. It was stupid, he knew; she was always with a team and almost always used the safety line and was probably a far more expert diver than Jess himself was. But what Jess couldn't see he couldn't control, and being required to stay with the boat while the others were underwater was the only thing Jess disliked about his job as captain.

The knot of anxiety that had formed in his stomach the minute she had gone in the water dissipated like magic when she broke the surface five minutes ahead of her scheduled time. Jess grinned when Simba appeared beside her, lifting herself to the rail for the stroke of Jess's hand.

"Don't do that!" Kelsey ordered, climbing the ladder. "The purpose of this project is *not* to resocialize her!"

"Lighten up," Jess advised mildly, helping her over the rail. "It's not doing any harm, and you're as bad as anybody else."

Dean surfaced on the other side of the boat. "Hey," he called. "I've got about forty minutes left in my tanks and ten minutes worth of film. I'm going to go down and see if I can give Craig a hand."

Kelsey tried to hide her annoyance as Jess helped her shrug out of her tanks. She and Dean had just spent twenty minutes filming and they could have used Craig's help. But he had scheduled his own experiment for the day, still searching for the elusive sleeping shark. It seemed to her that Craig was spending more time than ever on what was obviously a fruitless search. She said, "He's never going to find anything."

"Well, that's what we're here for—to look."

"What is it, about sixty feet?" She glanced at her watch, making rapid calculations for decompression time in her head, even though she knew Dean had already done so. "Okay, you need to start back at—"

"I know, Mom, I know." He replaced his face mask and mouthpiece, and pushed off against the side of the boat, back-flipping beneath the surface.

Kelsey pushed back her helmet and unzipped the wet suit, sitting down to take off her flippers. Simba circled the boat, enticing her to play, slapping her tail against the water, performing midair pirouettes. Kelsey tightened her lips grimly and ignored her.

Jess returned from stowing her air tanks just as she stood up to peel off the wet suit. He slipped his hands beneath the neck at the back to help her, his fingers warm against her sea-cooled skin. Kelsey stepped away.

"I can do it," she said, more sharply than she intended.

He lifted a querying eyebrow. "Bad day at the office, dear?"

"Don't give me a hard time, okay?" She swallowed hard as she tugged the material off her arms, pushed it down her legs. "I've got things on my mind."

"Like what?"

Like how to say goodbye to you in two days. Like how to start forgetting about you. Like how to concentrate on the job I'm supposed to be doing now when all I can think about is how little time we have left.... "If I wanted to talk I'd see a therapist," she said, stepping out of the suit and straightening the bottom of her swimsuit in the back. "I've got work to do."

"Don't be temperamental, Legs. I thought if there was one woman I could count on not to be temperamental, it was you."

"Don't call me that."

"What?"

"Legs. It's sexist and unprofessional."

"Like I'm not?"

But his tone lost its teasing as she pushed past him toward the storage lockers, her color high and her lips tight. "What's wrong?" he demanded quietly.

Kelsey opened the locker, arranged her wet suit inside with quick efficient motions, and had every intention of turning back into the wheelhouse to begin her recording of the day's events. But when she turned she heard herself crying instead, "Damn it, I need more time! Two weeks isn't enough!" *Not for me, not for us...*

She flung an impatient hand toward the bow, where Simba was splashing and chittering happily, enticing them to join her. "Look at that stupid dolphin! All our coming here has done is turn her back into a pet. Whatever good I did by reconditioning her to the wild is completely destroyed now and I haven't learned anything useful—nothing! If she does have a family she's too excited by the novelty of our being here to bring them to us, and if she's living alone there's no chance to observe her in her natural state because we're making everything *unnatural* and two weeks just isn't enough time to restore the balance. It isn't fair!''

"Do you want me to give you more time?'' he demanded, spreading his hands in a gesture of entreaty—or impatience. "If it were up to me, I would. You know that.''

She turned on him. "Would you?'' she challenged. "Would you really?''

And in that moment they both knew they weren't talking about dolphins or scientific experiments or two weeks at sea. And the moment seemed frozen between them—blue sky, sea breeze, creaking timbers, dolphin play—as they hovered suspended on the edge of recognition, confrontation and decision.

And then Jess said in a voice soft and tight with frustration, "Damn it, don't you think it's hard for me, too?''

Kelsey released an unsteady breath, overwhelmed with a surge of shame and uncertainty. She pushed a hand through her tangled hair. She glanced away briefly, then made herself meet his eyes again. "No man has ever been able to turn me into a raving lunatic before. I've got to hand it to you, you do have a way with women.''

She started toward the wheelhouse, and he intercepted her in two strides. His hand was firm on her arm, and even that touch, nonsexual as it was, made her stomach muscles weaken and her throat start to tighten.

She said with an effort, not looking at him, "Jess, don't, okay? This is hard enough as it is. I'm sorry I snapped at you. I just—this is hard. Let's just forget it.''

She started to pull away but his fingers tightened. He said "When we dock, it doesn't have to be the end you know.''

She caught her breath, blinking against a sudden stinging in her eyes, and she wasn't sure whether the stabbing sensation that went through the pit of her stomach was of hope or sorrow. She could feel his warmth all along her back, and his fingers strong on her arm. It was with all the willpower that she possessed that she kept herself from turning into his arms, and made herself shake her head.

"No," she said hoarsely. "There's no point in dragging it out.''

He released her arm slowly. "Hell, what difference would it make anyway?'' His voice was tired. "If I wasn't at sea you would be. We'd never see each other.''

Kelsey forced a tight smile. "See, that's what I like about sleeping with sailors. They never stay around long enough to get boring.''

He swung her around angrily. "Will you stop that? I hate it when you talk like that!''

And she jerked away, her eyes blazing. "What do you want me to do, marry you? For God's sake, Jess, get real! We are what we are and this is all we get!''

For a long moment they stared at each other, emotions seething, hasty words ringing in the air, the yearning between them so tight it practically snapped. A cloud passed over the sun and Simba, who had demonstrated a remarkable sensitivity to the moods of humans, had disappeared.

And then Kelsey said, subdued, "God, will you listen to us?"

Jess drew in a tight, frustrated breath, pushing his fingers through his hair. "I told you I was no good at relationships. I couldn't even keep a business partner around long enough to break even."

Kelsey dropped her eyes. "I wish we had more time," she whispered.

Jess lifted his hand, and cupped her neck. His eyes were bleak. "Me, too."

Kelsey placed her hands on his chest; she felt the softness of his T-shirt, the expansion of his muscles with a deep breath. She moved her hand down, over his heart. It was beating fast, like hers. She said, "I want to make love with you."

"Honey, we can't." His voice was a little hoarse, and he brought his hands up to cover hers, caressing her wrists. "The divers..."

"I don't care."

"Kelsey..."

But she didn't care. All she cared about at that moment was the desperate possessive need she felt for the body she knew so well and the man she hardly knew at all but felt she had known forever, the man she could never possess. She cared about the time they should have had and questions to which there were no answers and the solutions that didn't exist. She cared about him, and was storing up memories against the time when he would no longer be hers.

When she tugged her hands away from his and down the length of his body he didn't resist. She felt his sharp intake of breath as her fingers traced the shape of his nipples and then drifted downward, seeking the sensitive spot at the base of his spine. He smothered a moan and pushed his leg between her thighs, dropping his mouth to her neck. She closed her eyes, arching against the pleasure, moving her hands inside his shirt.

She whispered, "You know what I don't like about you? You don't have a tattoo."

"And you don't wear red satin underwear."

"So it's not . . . a match made in heaven."

"Not by a long shot."

But then his mouth covered hers and his hands clasped her bottom firmly, pressing her against his hardness. The passion flared in a matter of seconds, embers to flames, blinding and consuming. He swept her into his arms and somehow they were in the cabin, sunshine slicing across the bed and dancing off their bodies, flesh against flesh. She cried out when he entered her and dug her fingers into his shoulder, drawing him closer, holding him tighter. The rhythms they created were urgent, frantic, breathless; hands grasping, arms straining, mouths bruising as they desperately fought to hold on to what could never be theirs. And even as the physical pleasure exploded around them and sealed them together they clung harder to each other, holding on tightly until finally their trembling muscles forced them to let go.

They lay together, their bodies slick with perspiration, their breathing harsh, their arms and their legs entwined and their eyes closed tightly against the inevitable daylight reality, for a very long time. But the moments were stolen and couldn't last; they both knew that. Without a word, by mutual consent, they parted, and began to dress.

Jess knelt behind Kelsey on the bed, straightening the shoulder strap of her swimsuit. "It never helps, does it?" His voice was low, and strained. "Every time I make love with you I think this is the time the emptiness will go away, that the needing you will stop... but it doesn't. It just never gets any better."

"No," she whispered. "It doesn't."

He rested his cheek against her hair, his hand encircling her shoulder, and she let herself sink back into him, just one more time, just for a few minutes longer...

And then they heard something outside that made them both stiffen, and then leap to their feet. It was the frantic, screeching cry of a dolphin in distress.

They rushed to the deck just in time to see Simba make one final, agitated leap, then she dived and swam away from the boat with a speed that left a visible wake. "Jess!" Kelsey cried, running to the rail. In all the time she had worked with her, Kelsey had never seen the dolphin act like that, and it frightened her. "Jess, something's wrong! We have to—"

"Kelsey!" His voice was sharp and raw with alarm. "Starboard!"

When she reached him Jess was climbing over the rail, hand extended toward the water. It took both of them to get a gasping, pale-faced, badly shaken Dean aboard. Kelsey's heart was pounding frantically as she helped Jess remove Dean's air tanks, and when she met Jess's eyes in question his expression was grim.

"Balloon ascent," he said.

She turned on Dean, horrified. "Dean, are you crazy? What were you—"

"No choice," he gasped. And as soon as the tanks were removed his legs collapsed beneath him; he sank to the deck. "Shark—attack."

It was then that she noticed he was missing one flipper and a tiny rivulet of blood scored his ankle. A wave of ice went through Kelsey as she knelt beside him. "Craig," she said with an effort.

Dean shook his head, and after a moment caught his breath enough to reply. "He was—above me. Decompressing. I don't think . . . there were four or five of them. They were after me. I don't know why. This big mother—hammerhead—grabbed my flipper and if he hadn't it would've been my leg. I had no choice. I didn't want to leave him but I had—no choice."

Kelsey looked at Jess and she saw the same kind of dread in his eyes that was in hers. She closed her hand over Dean's. "It's okay. You did what you had to. I'll suit up."

She stood and Jess's hand closed around her arm, hard. He drew a breath and she knew what he was going to say, just as he knew what her answer would be and the struggle in his eyes hurt her and touched her and made her impatient and, in some strange way, glad. In the end all he said was, "We can't hang around here too long." He nodded toward Dean. "We've got to get him back in the water."

Dean said, "No, I'm okay, forget about me..." But his hands were shaking as he pushed back his helmet, and no color had returned to his face.

Kelsey went quickly to change.

Jess had her air tanks ready when she returned to the bow, and it was at that moment Craig broke the water. "Dean!" he cried. "Is he okay? My God, I never meant... Are you all right? Are you hurt?"

As he spoke he was climbing the ladder, with Jess's and Kelsey's help; now he knelt beside Dean. "There was nothing I could do, I couldn't get to you in time. If you'd waited I could have driven them away—"

Dean shook his head. "Forget it, they would've turned on you—"

"No, they wouldn't!" Craig exclaimed. He stood up, excitement shining in his eyes now that he saw Dean wasn't hurt, and began to strip off his tanks. "Don't you see, the suit works! They didn't touch me. I was right in the middle of them and they didn't even know I was there!"

Kelsey stared at him. "The suit? What are you talking about? You were supposed to—"

But Jess interrupted her with an odd warning look. "Start filling the tanks," he commanded quietly. "I'll take us out to deep water." And he swung toward the wheelhouse.

By the time Jess found a safe spot to anchor, Dean was already sweating and beginning to show signs of disorientation. Nitrogen narcosis—or "the bends," as it was commonly known—had taken hold quickly, and all they could do was take Dean back down to the depth at which he had begun his too-rapid ascent, and allow him to decompress gradually. Because natural decompression had been delayed and symptoms had already taken hold, returning the body to its correct balance took roughly ten times as long as it would have had Dean made a controlled ascent. They took turns staying with him: walking with him on the bottom, moving up a few feet, staying at that level, switching off when the air supply began to run low, working in perfect relay-team synchronization.

The process took the rest of the afternoon, and though the tedium was agony for everyone, Kelsey hardly noticed the passage of time.

She kept a sharp eye out for sharks, as did everyone else. They didn't see a single one. That would have been unusual under any circumstances; to spend as much time underwater as they, collectively, did that day in an area that was practically teeming with marine life of every description without catching so much as a glimpse of a shark was unlikely in the extreme. But what made it even more so was the near attack less than a mile distant. From Dean's description of the event, there was no discernible reason for such a number of sharks to gather in one spot, nor to be provoked into the kind of frenzy he had described. It didn't make any sense.

Simba, who had not been away from the boat for more than an hour or two since they had found her, did not return. Kelsey kept reassuring herself that the dolphin had shown no sign of injury before and was surely too smart to return to the area where the sharks had been. But she wished she could be sure.

She wished she could talk to Jess.

It was sunset by the time they were able to bring Dean safely on board. He was weak and exhausted, continually cursing himself for his misfortune and apologizing for the trouble, but he was out of danger. He went below and immediately fell asleep.

Jess, Craig and Kelsey were silent in their fatigue, putting together a makeshift meal, their conversation perfunctory and to the point. Craig kept looking as though he expected Kelsey to question him further about the attack, and he even offered her several openings. But Kelsey, thoughtful and distracted, ignored him.

It was full dark when she checked on Dean for the last time, and went back on deck. Craig was asleep, and she had not seen Jess in an hour. Simba had not returned.

The lights were on in the wheelhouse, and her steps were slow with weariness and dread as she went inside and sat down at the workstation. She turned on the radio receiver—the one they had used to track Simba's transmitter tag—and began to search other frequencies, hoping against hope that she would not find what she was looking for.

When she found it she swore viciously under her breath, and then sat there while fury and outrage wrestled with bitter resignation, and she knew what she had to do.

She went into her cabin to change into her wet suit, and when she came back out on deck Jess was there, lowering the dinghy into the water. She came over to him slowly.

"I figured you'd want to go after it tonight," he said. "I also figured you wouldn't want Craig to know what you were doing."

For a moment the emotions that washed through her were so intense they took away words. It was the feeling of not being alone, of being *known,* and of knowing another person so thoroughly that even their thoughts were in tandem. And it was a sense of surprise, and overwhelming wonder, because never had she expected such a thing, nor even imagined it, and she hardly knew how to feel at all. Except that in all her life she had never felt so safe, or important, or right. With Jess, for the first time in her life, she was connected to something outside herself and bigger than herself, and that thing was the two of them. And because of it, she would never be alone again. The recognition of that truth was staggering.

She managed after a moment, "How did you know?"

"It wasn't too hard to figure out. He wouldn't be the first fisherman to bait sharks with an electronic pulsator. Did you copy down the coordinates?"

She nodded. "And I'm bringing the receiver, just in case."

"Good."

He was wearing his wet suit, and the contours of his body rippled with each movement; moonlight glinted dully off his hair. Kelsey felt a sudden possessive stab of yearning for him that was so powerful it hurt.

He glanced at her. "You don't have to do this tonight," he said quietly. "There's a good chance he'll try to go back for the pulsator tomorrow...."

She shook her head firmly, leaning through the rail to drop her flippers into the dinghy. "I need it now. For..." And she swallowed hard. "Evidence."

She could feel his gaze on her, quiet and sympathetic, but she couldn't meet it. She climbed over the rail quickly and lowered herself into the smaller boat.

She lifted her arms to receive the set of air tanks he handed down to her. But then he passed her another set of tanks, and dropped down another pair of flippers. She stared at him as he climbed over the rail. "What do you think you're doing?"

"You were planning to tell me you were going, weren't you?"

She said a little uncertainly, "Well, of course, but—"

"And you weren't thinking about taking off in the dark like this by yourself?"

He dropped down beside her, then leaned forward to untie the anchor rope. She said, with difficulty, "I thought you didn't want to be a hero."

"Yeah, well it's kind of hard to avoid when you're in love with a thrill seeker."

Her pulses caught, then leaped into a new, faster rhythm. Everything within her tightened, suspended for a moment of aching expectation, and then she turned away.

When Jess pushed away from the boat she was already in position, and she silently handed him an oar.

Jess waited until they were out of sight of the boat to start the outboard, and then he ran it at its lowest possible speed—just enough to keep them on course, but hopefully not enough for the sound to carry back to the sleepers on board the *Miss Santa Fe*. Kelsey did not think there was anything Craig could do to stop them now, nor did she think he would even try, but she wasn't taking any chances.

After a time Jess spoke, his voice sober over the low hum of the outboard. "What's going to happen to him?"

Kelsey stared out into the night. The moon was bright enough to paint the ruffled sea with glitter, but still it was dark. Too dark. She said, "He'll be dismissed from the institute. He might be able to publish his findings, but his reputation will be destroyed. I suppose a criminal case could be made but I doubt Dean will pursue it."

"What about you?"

She said nothing.

"Well, I'm proud of you anyway."

Her voice was sharp. "For what?"

"Not going after him with that pistol of yours."

"You took it away from me, remember?" She tried to smile and failed. Her next words were heavy with defeat. "Anyway, I can't be mad at him when it's as much my fault as it is his."

"How do you figure?"

"I'm in charge of this expedition," she said tightly. "I'm the one who picked him for the team. I should've known a scientist of his caliber wouldn't waste time looking for sleeping sharks when he knew as well as I did what the odds were of finding them. I should have known the *only* thing he was interested in was proving that suit worked and I should've known we'd only left him one option in how to go about it. But I never get it right where people are concerned. *Never*. I should've known, and it's my fault."

"Right." His tone was relaxed and his hand easy on the tiller, his profile silvered by moonlight. "So is nuclear waste and street crime and the ozone layer. You can't be responsible for the whole world, Legs. If anybody should've figured out what the bastard was up to, it should've been me."

"You? Why in the world should you have known?"

He replied simply, "Because I'm the captain."

Kelsey looked at him for a moment longer, but the surge of affection and understanding that went through her was too much; she turned away.

"The suit doesn't work, you know," he went on after a moment. "So whatever profit Craig expected to make out of this is gone. Maybe that's punishment enough."

She turned back to him. "What do you mean, it doesn't work? You saw yourself..." But even as she spoke, she began to understand.

"The way I figure it," Jess explained unnecessarily, "it was a combination of the pulsator and whatever electronic masking the suit was doing that put the sharks into such a frenzy. It was confusion, more than anything else, that made them attack Dean. If Dean hadn't been there, unprotected, they would've eventually found Craig."

"That's right," Kelsey agreed thoughtfully. "That's why the suit didn't work in lab conditions—because nobody was in the water with him to distract the sharks. So his findings are invalidated, no matter what else happens." And she sighed, rubbing a wary hand over her face. "I should have figured that out, too."

Jess glanced at her, and his smile was as bracing as a caress. "That's what you've got me around for."

She wanted to smile back, but she couldn't. The sea below them was so dark, the night around them so vast, and she could not look at Jess without aching inside. She said, "I usually get things right. I've spent a lifetime making sure I was always right... but everything about this trip has been a mistake, right from the start. I had so much riding on it, and now—one man's career is ruined, another almost got himself killed, and I haven't accomplished anything. All the planning, all the preparation, all the work... and all I've got is 'findings inconclusive.'"

"You must be tired." Jess eased back on the throttle as he checked the compass. "I've only been in this business two weeks and even I can see you've proven something pretty important.''

He turned against the wind, and the breeze whipped Kelsey's hair across her face. She caught it back impatiently with one hand. "Oh, yeah, what's that?"

"That the bond the dolphin formed with humans is more important to her than anything she could have with her own kind. She loves you, Legs. And I think she wants to stay with you.''

Kelsey stared at him, thinking of a dozen dismissing comments and rejecting each one before it could be spoken. That was not what she had set out to prove, not at all. It wasn't even a scientific theory. And yet... there *was* a possibility there. There was definitely something to explore.

She murmured, thinking out loud, "Now *that* would make a television documentary, wouldn't it? Of course, it's not something you could prove in a couple of weeks. I'd need a lot more time to expose her to other stimuli, to study her responses to different situations..." And then she stopped and shook her head. "No, it's ridiculous. Anyway, the point of this whole project was to *undo* her human bonds. I wanted her to be free.''

Jess's gaze was soft and steady across the narrow space between them. "Maybe," he suggested, "free isn't always the best thing to be."

She knew he wasn't simply talking about dolphins, and the knowledge confused her, and disoriented her a little, making her ache inside for something she didn't understand and couldn't begin to define. After a moment she looked away, and she said, with difficulty. "Anyway, it might not matter. She's never been gone this long before."

Jess had no answer for that.

He navigated the small craft across the empty ocean as easily as though he were negotiating a superhighway, and cut the engine within a hundred feet of where the radio receiver showed the transmitter to be—a feat that even Kelsey had to admire. They used the oars to position themselves precisely above the pulsator, and Jess said, "There's an outcropping about twenty feet down we can tie off on. I'll hook a spotlight underneath the boat and we should be able to follow it straight down."

She cast him an appreciative glance as she pulled on her flippers. "You do know your waters."

"You hired an expert, you get an expert."

But as he bent down to pull on his flippers Kelsey reached across and stayed his hand. "Jess," she said, trying hard to keep the urgency out of her voice. "Stay with the boat. There's no need for both of us to go down—"

He shook his head, not even glancing up. "Forget it, Legs."

Her hand tightened. "Jess, there're sharks down there."

And then he looked up at her. "It's also dark down there."

For a moment their gazes held, and the message that passed between them was as strong and as tender as an embrace. And then, because they had no choice, they turned back to the business at hand.

Jess checked her regulator, and she checked his. They strapped on their dive belts, secured their helmets, pulled on gloves. As a last precaution, they each fastened on safety lines.

"There's about a hundred feet of line here," Jess said. His voice was tight, and as hollow as she felt inside. "I figure the pulsator to be about sixty-five or seventy feet down, so for God's sake, don't get fouled."

She nodded. "Check your dive light."

He did, and so did she.

The last thing Jess picked up was a bang stick—a long electronic club, like an underwater cattle prod. It was almost always effective in deterring sharks. Almost always.

Dread was like a cold fist in Kelsey's stomach as she looked at him. "I really don't want to do this," she said.

He agreed bleakly, "Neither do I."

But they couldn't delay much longer. He checked the spotlight, reached for his face mask. Kelsey touched his arm. "Jess..."

He looked at her.

"I do love you," she said.

She pulled up her face mask, and stepped into the water.

Ten

Gravity sucked her down into the blackness for what seemed like forever before she stopped herself with a turn, and kicked back toward what she hoped was the surface. There was always that moment of disorientation; an instant when she couldn't tell up from down or right from left and the darkness took her breath away. It seemed forever that she fumbled with her dive light, fighting the inky water, trying not to breathe too hard ... and then a milky light poured down from above her, and Jess touched her arm.

There was no describing what she felt at that moment, when the darkness went away and he was there, but she knew she would remember it, and carry it with her like a talisman, for the rest of her life. He touched her, and she was calm. He looked at her and she was strong. She wasn't alone anymore.

He held her eyes for a moment, and her lips tightened around the mouthpiece, fighting a smile, when she realized he was also watching her bubbles, measuring the pace of her breathing. She held up her thumb and forefinger to him, making an okay sign, and he winked at her behind the face mask. He held up the mooring line from the dinghy and pointed west. She nodded and followed him, switching on her dive light to guide him as they moved out of the circle of the spotlight.

The rock outcropping was where he said it would be. They secured the boat against drift and started down, following the direction of the ever-fading spotlight.

The world around them was painted in shades of gray, silent and still, and though Kelsey knew the ocean was teeming with life it seemed to her that she and Jess were the only two creatures who lived in all the universe. And the strange thing was that it was enough. As long as Jess was beside her, his body strong and sleek as it pushed downward with her into the depths, she wasn't afraid.

He kept close to her, his hand brushing her hip. And with two lights, the darkness was easier to combat.

The deeper they swam the tighter Kelsey's anxiety grew. The darkness was solid except for the narrow swatch cut by their flashlights, and she tried not to think about the things that could be lurking there in the darkness, about how easy it would be to become separated from Jess, to lose her safety line, to become so helplessly disoriented she couldn't even find the surface... She wouldn't think about that but she couldn't avoid thinking about the fact that they were moving, with every breath, deeper into danger, closer to an area that had been deliberately baited for sharks—and that at last notice, those sharks had been in a frantic attack mode. She thought about Dean, an experienced marine worker, who had been forced into a balloon ascent that could have killed him. And she thought about Jess, with his admitted phobia. If he panicked, how could she help him? If either of them was attacked, what could the other do? The only weapon they had between them was one bang stick, frail enough at best. They didn't even know how many sharks were circling. And the dark was getting thicker and deeper...

Suddenly she thought, quite clearly, *This is crazy.* It wasn't worth it. Jess was risking his life for her; they *both* were risking their lives and for what? A principle. Another man's foolishness, a misguided sense of self-importance... No, it wasn't worth it. Not now, when for the first time in her life she had found something more important than her own ambitions, more important than being right, more important than winning. Not now, when she had just found Jess.

She moved in front of him in the water and turned, wanting to signal to him to begin an ascent. But he caught her arm and pointed.

She swung her light in the direction of his and saw the pulsator resting on the ocean floor.

She signaled him to stay where he was, and she swam down to it. His light never left her.

She had the pulsator in her hand when suddenly the light dimmed, interrupted by a shadow that cut across the night. She turned and staggered back as a sleek gray body brushed against her; a gasp of shock and fear clouded the water with a fog of bubbles, and she dropped the pulsator without ever getting a chance to turn it off.

It all happened in a matter of moments, yet retained that horrible slow-motion clarity characteristic of nightmares . . . or of real life in sixty feet of water. The tiger shark, six feet of perfectly engineered predator, swung around Kelsey in a leisurely maneuver, beginning to circle. She fumbled for the pulsator, knowing that even if she found it and turned it off it would be too late. She saw Jess's face as he lunged for her, his expression grim and intent against the distorting mask of water, and she wanted to scream *No! No, get back, one of us is all it wants, go back!*

Jess veered toward the shark, and she knew the courage it cost him to do so. The stream of bubbles that surrounded him was just as panicked as her own. He thrust his bang stick toward the shark and it veered away, then turned to lunge toward Jess.

Kelsey screamed, silently and helplessly as the shark charged Jess. She saw him thrust the stick toward the shark again and then saw the stick tumble out of his hand. And suddenly they were not alone.

At first Kelsey thought it was another shark and horror left her paralyzed. Then the dolphin darted

between Jess and the attacking shark and a new kind
of horror overcame her and she tried to scream—as
experienced as she was, as practical and knowledge-
able as she was, she actually tried to scream the warning—*Simba!* But it was over so quickly; the entire
episode took only a few breaths.

Jess staggered back and Simba dived upward with
one of those amazing bursts of speed and agility dolphins are known to display, then down again in front
of the shark, darting away as the shark turned and
lunged. Jess grabbed the bang stick; he thrust it
against the shark's side viciously. The shark darted
away. Jess thrust again. Simba dived behind him. The
shark seemed to waver, disoriented. Kelsey at last
found the pulsator and turned it off. Jess struck the
shark again. The shark retreated.

Kelsey swam toward him, trying not to waste air
with the sharp breaths of sobs or laughter that were
tearing at her throat, but she couldn't help it. The water swirled between them as they came together,
grasping each other's arms in the only way they could
embrace, holding on tightly. Not even the wavering
mask of water nor the shifting, swirling patterns of
darkness could disguise the emotions on their faces
then, nor the intensity that fired their eyes.

And when Simba appeared again out of the darkness, nudging against them with playful affection,
Kelsey was glad, for the first time since it had all begun, to be underwater. Had she not been, and ham-
pered by the face mask and breathing apparatus, she
was sure she would have burst into tears of sheer joy.

* * *

Jess climbed into the dinghy first, then leaned over to help Kelsey in. She took off her air tanks and handed them to him, then grasped his arms as he lifted her over the edge of the boat and inside. She fell against him, and he didn't let go. He caught her face in his hands and his mouth covered hers; they drank of each other desperately, hungrily, with all the joy and triumph that was life itself, for an endless time.

When they parted his hands remained on her face and her eyes remained riveted on his; they looked at each other, adoring each other. Kelsey said softly, "That was some pretty fancy shark fighting."

His eyes crinkled with a smile. "Yeah, it was, wasn't it?"

Simba stretched out of the water, chittering for attention, and Kelsey laughed, moving to stroke the dolphin with both hands. "For both of you!"

Jess joined her, stretching out his hand to caress the dolphin's head. "You can call your project a failure if you want, lady, but you're looking at one sailor who's damn glad this dolphin has a soft spot in her heart for humans. And as far as I'm concerned, the mackerel is on me for the rest of her life."

Almost as though she understood, Simba flipped and splashed the water joyfully. Kelsey and Jess stumbled back in the boat, laughing. They knelt with their arms around each other, watching as Simba circled the dinghy once, then swam away. Smiling tenderly, Jess reached up and pushed back Kelsey's helmet, freeing her hair, tangling his fingers in it for a moment. Then he said, "I think maybe she's got the right idea. Let's get out of here."

He started the outboard, and Kelsey knelt in the stern, tilting her head back to the cool sea breeze, watching for glimpses of Simba's dorsal fin glinting in the moonlight in the distance.

Jess said, "What are you going to do about Craig?"

Kelsey turned slowly, some of the exhilaration on her face fading into thoughtfulness, even somberness. "I don't want to ruin the man," she said, after a moment. "I don't think he meant for anybody to get hurt. If he had told us what he was doing no one would have gotten hurt—but he couldn't tell us, because I wouldn't have approved it. He was desperate, he did what he thought he had to, and he was wrong. Maybe you're right. Maybe that's punishment enough." She released a breath. "He'll have to leave the institute. But beyond that . . . we'll have to talk."

Jess smiled at her, and said nothing. She had never imagined that any man's approval would mean so much to her, nor that something so simple as a smile could draw her as close as an embrace.

She said hesitantly, searching his eyes, "Jess . . . tonight, I wasn't afraid."

He nodded, his expression softened with understanding. "It makes a difference when you're not alone, doesn't it?"

She said softly, "Yes." Because, although she had been underwater and in the dark with many partners before, until tonight she had always been alone. *He* was the difference. It was that simple.

She turned her head to look out over the sea again, and smiled as a shaft of moonlight danced across Simba's arching back. "Do you really think it's true, what you said before? About... freedom not always being the best thing?"

He answered, "Are we talking about dolphins, here?"

Kelsey caught her breath, and turned to look at him. Her heart was beating slowly and heavily and every nerve in her body tingled with an uncertain expectation. "I don't know. Are we?"

She thought no man had ever looked as beautiful as he did at that moment: his hair, curled by the wind and silvered with moonlight, his form strong and straight, his eyes as deep as the ocean floor and just as unfathomable as he looked at her. He said, very carefully, "Of course, neither one of us is the kind to ever be tied down to one harbor."

Kelsey tried to make her heart stop pounding, and her throat to stop aching. "No," she managed, and looked away. "We're not."

For a long time there was nothing but the hum of the motor and the gentle slapping sound the small craft made against the water. The salt breeze stung Kelsey's eyes and her chest hurt with the force of emotions, inexplicable and unspeakable, that were welling up inside her. And then, abruptly, Jess cut the motor. There was no sound at all other than ocean sounds, no movement except the drift of the tide. Kelsey turned slowly, staring at him.

Then he spoke again, his voice easy and matter-of-fact. "So here's the proposition. I made out a little better on that partnership split than I might have led you to believe. I've got some money—not a lot, but some. More importantly, I've got a boat. A pretty good start on that floating lab of yours."

Kelsey's heart was pounding again, so hard she could barely hear herself speak, or keep her voice steady. "You'd—give up your business for me?"

He gave a derisive shake of his head. "I wouldn't be giving up anything. I'd be gaining what I've always wanted—twenty-four hours a day at sea."

Her mind was racing, her head spinning, her heart pounding. The possibilities leaped and danced and cascaded just beyond her reach, a lifetime ambition, a dream come true...yet she wasn't thinking about the lab, or the boat, or a business deal. She was thinking about Jess. Twenty-four hours a day with Jess. A lifetime with Jess. Possibilities with Jess... It would never work. How could it work? She was crazy to even consider it, he was crazy to mention it...but she wanted it to work. They could make it work. It *had* to work.

And in the end all she could say was, "But—you hate partners."

"Yeah," he agreed, "but I guess that's something I'm going to have to get over. Because there's a condition to my offer." He turned then, and looked fully at her. She heard his indrawn breath, she saw the tautness around his eyes. "You have to marry me."

She stopped breathing. It was as though someone had struck her in the solar plexus; she literally could not draw a breath, and by the time she was able to do so her lungs were burning and her throat was bursting. She brought an unsteady hand to her lips; she had to look away. "Jess, don't." Her voice was low, and broken. "Don't make me answer that...."

He moved closer to her, reaching for her hand, removing it from her face. He made her look at him. "Listen," he said hoarsely. "This is the hardest thing I've ever done. And the craziest. Harder, and crazier, than fighting sharks. But if I can ask, the least you can do is think about it. And while you are thinking, think about this. You were afraid of the water, so you became a marine biologist. You were afraid of caves, so you became an expert cave diver. All your life you've been afraid of getting close to someone, just like I've been. The only way for either one of us to get over that is to become an expert at relationships. And the best way to do that is by getting married."

She couldn't stop staring at him. She could hardly get her breath. And the worst thing was that what he said almost made sense.

"I love you, too, Kelsey," he said gently. "And I want to stay with you."

She dragged her eyes away, pulling in a breath, forcing her head into a negative motion. "No, it's crazy. You don't know what you're saying. I'm no good at this, Jess, you know that. I've been wrong from the beginning—about Craig, about Simba, about you... What if I'm wrong now? About the way I feel, about the way I think you feel—''

His hand tightened on hers, and he brought her curled fingers to his cheek, sandpaper rough, briny damp. ''The only thing you've been right about,'' he corrected huskily, ''is me. From that first night, it was like lightning, and we both knew it.''

She looked back at him helplessly, and she knew all she felt was written in her eyes. Lighting. More than that; it was wizardry, magic, the impossible brought to life. How could she deny that? How could either of them? But... ''We hardly know each other,'' she said, casting about in confusion. Her heart had picked up a new, excited rhythm that she didn't understand.

''Right,'' he agreed, rubbing the back of her fingers lightly over his stubbled chin. ''Two weeks isn't much time. But I've thought about it, and I'm not going to feel any differently about you in two more weeks, or two years, or twenty... You'll still make me mad and you'll still make me crazy and you'll still be the only real woman I've ever known in my life.''

He dropped his eyes then, studying their entwined fingers. ''I think,'' he said soberly, ''that other people can afford excuses like that. They can shop around, take their time...but for people like you and me, Kelsey, it only comes once. And we have to grab it while we can.''

Then Kelsey knew why her heart was beating so, why the excitement was swelling inside her—because there was only one answer she could give him. And she had known it all along.

She lifted their entwined fingers to her lips, smiling against his touch. "Of course," she murmured, "I do get along with you better than I ever thought I could with any man, and the sex is—"

"Nuclear meltdown."

"Armageddon."

"Unforgettable."

"Right."

His eyes held hers, sparking with joy and certainty, moonlight dancing on the water. The wonder that swelled inside her made her dizzy, and left her weak. "I never loved a man before, Jess," she said softly. "I'm afraid I might not do it right."

He lifted his hand and caressed her hair, smoothing it against the breeze. "I think," he said slowly, "that you and I are probably the only two people in the world who can say 'I've never loved before' and mean it. We were lucky to find each other, Kelsey. And that's what scares me, because that kind of luck is too good to be true. I don't want to take a chance on losing you."

Kelsey sat there, rubbing her aching throat, bursting with things to say to him and unable to put any of them into words. Finally she said, "We're so much alike. We'd be at each other's throats all the time. How could we live together?"

And he answered simply, "Easier than we could live apart."

She knew it was true. She knew it was right, she knew it was crazy and she knew she had no choice . . .

she hadn't had one since the moment she had first seen him walking down the dock.

She kissed his fingers, hiding a smile, and released them. She said, "I have to think about it."

He replied, with a rather unsettling equanimity, "Okay." He started up the motor again and resumed their course.

He pulled up alongside the *Miss Santa Fe* and she helped him tie off. She climbed the ladder first and he handed the equipment up to her. And it wasn't until he climbed up on deck beside her that she saw how taut his face was, his eyes dark with anxiety behind the assumed calm. And she almost smiled.

She began to peel out of her wet suit, and so did he. It was close to midnight and she should have been exhausted; instead every muscle in her body was singing with energy. She had yet to confront Craig, and it would not be easy. But tomorrow would be soon enough for that, and Jess would be by her side. Tomorrow, too, they should head for shore. It would be hard to leave the sea behind but she had taken this phase of the project as far as she could, and going home would be easier, with Jess by her side.

She slipped her arms out of the sleeves of the wet suit and this time she didn't object when Jess slipped his fingers inside the material at the waist, tugging it down over her hips, her legs, her feet. When she had divested herself of the garment he settled his hands around her waist and pulled her gently back against him. She could feel his bare thighs against the backs of hers, his swimsuit and hers the only barriers separating them.

As always, every cell sprang to awareness of his touch, her breathing quickened and her pulses began to dance. But she kept her voice admirably steady as she said, "Okay, I've thought about it."

Jess went very still.

She took a breath. "There's just one condition. I get to be the captain."

He relaxed, turning her in his arms. "No chance." But his eyes were dancing, sparkling with the light of a thousand stars buried in the sea.

"It's my project!"

"It's my boat."

"But—"

He covered her mouth with a kiss, and she sank into it, lifting her arms around his neck, clinging to him; needing him, loving him, wanting to move worlds for him and feeling as though she could . . . and yet still afraid to try.

"Oh, Jess," she whispered against his neck, holding him tightly. "I want this to be right. But what if we can't? What if we don't know how? What if we make a mistake?"

He took her hands from around his neck, folding them together, holding them just beneath his chin. He looked at her soberly. "We'll make mistakes," he said. "Lots of them. And we'll just keep trying till we get it right. I want you to know, Kelsey, you're one of the few things I've ever known that's worth fighting for. I'll do whatever it takes."

She released one of her hands and stroked his cheek. "I'm not sure you know what you're getting into."

He smiled. "I'm not sure you do."

"No," she said thoughtfully. "I think maybe we both know exactly what we're getting into. And *that's* what makes us crazy."

He laughed softly, and so did she, and their lips met in a brief and gentle kiss.

He took a small step back, looking down at her. "I'll tell you what. Maybe we can share the captain's duties."

"And privileges?"

"Of course."

She studied him thoughtfully for a moment. "I guess I can live with that. As long as we both know who's boss."

He grinned as he drew her into his arms again. "Oh, I think we both know that."

*   *   *   *   *

COMING IN AUGUST FROM

Silhouette Desire

The Case of the Mesmerizing Boss

DIANA PALMER

Diana Palmer's exciting new series begins in August with THE CASE OF THE MESMERIZING BOSS...

Dane Lassiter—one-time Texas Ranger *extraordinaire*—now heads his own group of crack private detectives. Soul-scarred by women, this heart-stopping private eye exists only for his work—until the night his secretary, Tess Meriwether, becomes the target of drug dealers. Dane wants to keep her safe. But their stormy past makes him the one man Tess doesn't want protecting her...

Don't miss THE CASE OF THE MESMERIZING BOSS by Diana Palmer, first in a lineup of terrific heroes! In November, watch for THE CASE OF THE CONFIRMED BACHELOR... only from Silhouette Desire!

COMING NEXT MONTH

ISN'T IT ROMANTIC?
Kathleen Korbel

Sexy newsman Pete Cooper couldn't refuse to fulfil his zany aunt's last request. But was it all some mischievous plan to get Brooke Ferguson into his arms?

UNEARTHLY DELIGHTS
Karen Leabo

Alicia Bernard was barely five foot two, but she wasn't going to be intimidated by six feet of lean, stubborn male. If Dom Seeger thought he could scare her off his archaeological dig, he had better think again!

BOSS LADY
Jackie Merritt

Pregnant widow TJ Reese was desperate for a right-hand man to help run her construction business. Zach Torelli was competent, trustworthy and *gorgeous*. How was she going to convince him that their relationship must stay strictly business?

Silhouette Desire

COMING NEXT MONTH

HOMETOWN MAN
Jo Ann Algermissen

Caroline Noble was returning to the town that had
scorned her. She was coming back a wealthy
woman and she wanted the town's respect. Lee
Carson had come from the wrong side of town, too,
but he'd never run from his roots. And he'd never
stopped wanting Caroline...

MOONLIGHT PROMISE
Noelle Berry McCue

Outwardly they were the perfect couple—handsome,
successful, loving. But Tricia had married Marcus
knowing he wanted them to live separate lives, and
sleep in separate beds. Why?

DREAM MENDER
Sherryl Woods

September's *Man of the Month*, expert carpenter
Frank Chambers, was sexy, stubborn...and solitary,
until Jenny Michaels came into his life. But pretty
Jenny had some secrets of her own...